HUMP'S FIRST CASE

Also by Ralph Dennis
The War Heist

The Hardman Series
Atlanta Deathwatch
The Charleston Knife is Back in Town
The Golden Girl And All
Pimp For The Dead
Down Among The Jocks
Murder Is Not An Odd Job
Working For The Man
The Deadly Cotton Heart
The One Dollar Rip-Off
Hump's First Case
The Last Of The Armageddon Wars
The Buy Back Blues

HUMP'S FIRST CASE

RALPH DENNIS

ISBN: 1941298834
ISBN-13: 978-1-941298-83-1

Published by Brash Books, LLC
12120 State Line #253
Leawood, Kansas 66209
www.brash-books.com

PUBLISHER'S NOTE

This book was originally published in 1977 and reflects the cultural and sexual attitudes, language, and politics of the period.

CHAPTER ONE

It was bitter-ass cold. It was a week before Christmas and the early-morning temperatures the last three days had been down in the teens. It wasn't much better in the sunlight. It wasn't the usual Atlanta weather.

I'd just had dinner at my girlfriend's apartment. Marcy had done a couple of pounds of veal some Italian way, with garlic and lemon and olive oil. I'd taken a good bottle of a Graves with me and we'd had the last glass of it in the bedroom. It was a good-bye-for-now party. Early the next morning she was flying up to Washington to spend a few days with an uncle and aunt, the last of her family. She wouldn't be back until Christmas Eve. I'd left about ten-thirty so that she could do the rest of her packing and get a few hours' sleep. Driving home I could feel the just-before-Christmas depression settling in. It would be worse with her out of town.

I was almost home when I remembered that I didn't have anything for breakfast. Not even eggs, not even bread. I made a turn and headed for the nearest 7–11 store. I got there about ten minutes before closing time. There were two cars parked out front, a battered white VW and a cream-colored convertible, a Mercury that was probably a 1957.

Inside I went straight for the bread rack. It was all that puffed-air stuff, the kind of bread I hate. But I picked out a loaf and held it carefully by the tied end. A few ounces of pressure and it would compress into a ball about the size of a biscuit. I got a dozen eggs from the dairy shelf and I was leaning over, staring down at the packages of bacon, when I realized that something was wrong.

I guess it was the old habits. The trained feelings that came from the time I'd been a cop. That had been years ago but I still had those instincts. Without turning around, I ran it through my head one more time.

There'd been a young girl behind the counter near the cash register. Long blond hair and blue eyes. Wrong thing number one: she'd been wearing a sheepskin jacket. Behind the counter? Unless, of course, she was ready to close for the night, waiting out those last ten minutes.

And the two young men. One stood with an elbow on top of the cash register. He was tall and thin, hair worn in a neat and short white afro. The other young man stood to his right, at the counter where you placed the items you were buying. He'd had a stack of six or seven cans of cat food. A heavy young man. Dark hair in what used to be called a ducktail. A denim jacket with a huge Budweiser patch on the back of it.

I'd seen that and I'd lost myself in trying to find a package of bacon that wasn't green around the edges.

And then the rest of it went wrong. I heard the bell on the front door. I stood and turned. The girl and the two men were going out the door. The two men were a few steps ahead, the girl trailing them. I yelled, "Hey, who do I pay for this?"

The girl whirled and I saw the paper bag in her hand. She stared at me with wide eyes and shook her head. The headshaking looked like a warning. She sprinted toward the Mercury convertible. The passenger-side door was open. She got in and pulled it closed. The driver burned rubber getting out of the parking lot.

I walked to the counter and placed the eggs and the bread next to the cash register. I looked over my shoulder and saw that the cash-register drawer was open.

Then I got the smell. The smell of dead.

A woman about thirty sprawled on the floor behind the counter. She'd been shot at least twice, once in the head and once in the chest. I knew better but I circled the counter and tried for a pulse. There wasn't one.

"And you just stood there?"

That was the young detective from Robbery. I didn't know him. He'd come up after I'd left. His last name was Ellison and I hadn't caught his first name.

I gave him a tired look. "You know who I am?"

"I know who you are," he said. The way he said it was like spitting out something that had been trapped between your teeth for a couple of days.

Those years gone and I guess they still used me as a scare story, one they could point out to the young cops and say, If you don't watch out you'll end up like Jim Hardman. "You know that much," I said; "you know I don't work as a cop anymore."

He broke the stare first. He looked down at what he'd written. Cream-colored Mercury, maybe a 1957. "You get the tag numbers?"

"No."

"You're a lot of help."

"I called you," I said. "I've given you a description of the three of them. That's about all I can do as a citizen who's not licensed to carry iron. You get me a gun permit and the next time I walk into a situation like this I'll blow the scumbags away."

"You talk rough," Ellison said.

"I feel rough. Somebody just spoiled my night's sleep."

He closed his notebook. "I might need you to look at some mug shots."

"That would be a big waste of time. Those three were about one step past being juveniles. If they've got records, they've been sealed by the court."

"A lineup if I find them?"

I nodded. He wheeled away. I stood at the counter and looked at the loaf of bread and the carton of eggs. No change in the register and the executive from 7–11, the one the police had called, didn't seem interested in sales. I dropped the bread on the shelf and returned the eggs to the refrigerator case. There went breakfast.

Passing the counter, on the way out, I heard Ellison ask the 7–11 man if he knew how much was missing from the register. He answered that he'd have to close out the register after the print man was done with it, but they'd started with a hundred in change and ...

"One of the guys took some cans of cat food," I said.

They looked at me like I was crazy.

"Six or eight cans of it," I said.

I knew better. I wasn't crazy. Screw them. I made the longer drive to Ansley Mall and did my shopping at the Kroger's that remained open all night. I got everything I needed. The bread was Arnold's Brick Oven and the bacon wasn't green.

The next day the afternoon paper, *The Journal,* carried a write-up on the robbery on an inside page of the front section. It said the dead woman had been Emma Jean Peters and she'd been thirty-one years old. There wasn't any mention of me. That was the way I liked it. Low profile and all that.

That evening, depressed by all the Christmas advertising and all that *Jingle Bells* crap on the radio, I did a lowlife tour with Hump Evans. We started in some strip joints and ended up at the singles bars far out Peachtree Road.

Hump draws a lot of attention wherever he goes. He's six-six or seven and weighs in at 270 or so. He's midnight black and he used to play a hell of a defensive end at Cleveland before he tore up a knee in a pileup and lost a step of quickness. Right now he's still seven times quicker than I am.

The singles bars were meat on the table and all out front. Not an ounce of coy to it. A lot of the women had their eyes on Hump. Most of the women looked at me like I carried plague germs. I guess I'm their old-age nightmare. Pudgy and mid-forties, reflecting what they are or what they'll be in a few years.

Midnight, with drink sloshing in me, I left Hump to choose his meat from the buffet and drove home. I showered and brushed my teeth. The shower was to wash off all the perfume and the stench of men's cologne that I felt I'd sucked up in those bars. The teeth brushing to erase the taste of one more rejection.

I was ready for bed when the doorbell rang. I put on a pair of khaki slacks and a clean T-shirt and went to the door barefooted. The board parts of the floor were like ice-skating without shoes.

Probably Hump. But you couldn't be sure. Not sure enough to go to the door in boxer shorts. I unlocked the door and swung it open. The porch was dark. Waves of condensed breath swirled past me. With that came the delicate scent of some perfume and the harshness of some no-nonsense men's aftershave.

I flipped on the porch light. A couple stood there. They were around my age. The man was short and bull-chested, with a jaw like a rock and a thin mouth. He had dark hair with a band of gray that ran up his sideburns and into the hair over his ears.

The woman on his right was three or four inches taller than he was. Maybe five-ten or eleven. She'd been a beauty in her time and that time wasn't too many years past. She had a model's lean and almost bony face. Green innocent eyes. Dark hair with the beauty-shop-gray streaking.

"Yeah?" The doorway was like a wind tunnel.

"You're James Hardman?" I heard the accent and I knew right away that he wasn't a redneck. It was northern, New York or somewhere like that.

"That's me." My eyes slid from him to the woman. She was staring down at my bare feet. At the toenails that needed clipping and the soap yellowing that formed on the nails. Once a month Marcy would get after me about showering so hurriedly.

The woman said, "We're Billie Joe's parents."

I'd expected the same accent from her. Hers wasn't northern. It was southern and soft and musical. Not Tidewater or Charleston. Not the fancy ones. This was small-town country with a pinch of polish tossed in. "I don't know him."

"It's not a him," the woman said.

"Her," the man corrected me.

"Billie Joe's the girl at the 7–11 store," the woman said.

"I know it's late," the man said. "We'll apologize for that ahead of time. But we've just arrived in Atlanta today and we've tried to call you all evening."

"The blond girl?" I backed from the doorway and waved them inside. The woman passed first. The perfume rubbed against me and replaced what I'd just washed off. He followed and, along with the shaving lotion, there was the smell of tweed and pipe tobacco.

I closed the door and switched off the porch light. "Have a seat. I'll put on my shoes." On the way past the thermostat I pushed and slapped at it until I heard the furnace cut in. The bedroom door shut behind me, I put on socks, shoes and a shirt. When I returned to the living room they were still standing, coats on, looking at each other. "I feel better in the kitchen. How about some coffee or a drink or coffee and a drink?"

"The kitchen sounds good," she said. I caught a look of gentle amusement. Yes, there was some backwoods in that girl or maybe it was a memory from a long time ago. From a time when, if there was a living room, it was for show. The kitchen was the center of the house.

I led the way. I filled the kettle and placed it on the burner. I got down three shot glasses and an unopened bottle of

Courvoisier that I'd bought myself as an early Christmas present. While I used a knife to cut the foil away, I looked at them. They'd removed their coats and left them in the living room. He wore Harris tweed, about two hundred dollars worth of jacket. She wore a gray knit dress. Her body looked real, heated, a burn to the touch.

"What makes you think it's your daughter?"

"Actually she's my stepdaughter," he said. He'd pulled out a chair for her. Now he eased it in. "Do you have the picture, Rosemary?"

"Yes, Charles." She was about to place her bag on the floor next to the chair legs. Now she lifted it, opened the clasp, and took out a photo that looked about four by six. She passed the picture to him and he looked at it and turned to hand it to me. I shook my head. I was pouring the cognac. He waited until I finished that. I gave it a brief look and dropped it on the table so that I could pass the brandy around.

"Mister ..." I stopped.

He gave a flustered laugh. "That's not like me. We've barged in on you and we haven't even introduced ourselves."

"It's been a bad time for you, Charles."

"That's true. I'm Charles Atkinson and this is Rosemary."

"I don't know what it is ..." I broke it off and shook my head. I didn't know what the hell was going on and I wasn't sure I could say that it was a pleasure to meet them.

"This is an imposition," Charles said.

I watched him. There was a kind of hesitation. I had the feeling he was about to pick up the photo, get their coats and leave.

"Forget it," I said. "I'm not being reasonable. We've gone this far. Let's go the rest of the way." I had a sip of the cognac and picked up the picture. It had the graininess of a blowup and parts of the original had been sliced away.

The girl in the photo wore a ball gown. It was white and lacy and low cut, with the cleavage and the upward roundness of young breasts. On both sides of her there was the suggestion of a dark arm or shoulder. Her hair was blond and short, barely to her chin. I stared at the face, the shape of it, and closed my eyes. I tried to hold that shape and add the longer hair I'd seen in the 7-11 store. It wasn't entirely a success. The face the night before had been thinner. Still, just before it faded, there was enough of a fuzzy match to make me think it might be a possibility.

"When was the picture taken?"

"This summer," Charles Atkinson said.

"At the Cotillion," Rosemary said.

"It's a debutante ball," he said.

That explained what had been cut away. The arms and shoulders had been those of her escorts for the evening. "Do you have a photo of her with longer hair?"

"No." Rosemary looked at her husband. "She never wore her hair long ... until now."

Charles had a sip of the brandy. He held it on his tongue for a long time before he swallowed. "Do you think it was Billie Joe in that store last night?"

"I'm not sure. It could be. If she's wearing her hair longer now, if she's lost some of the baby fat from her face."

"I knew it," Rosemary said. "I just knew it."

"Look," I said. "I didn't say that at all. What I said was that it could have been."

"But you didn't say that it definitely wasn't her." Charles looked at me above the rim of the glass.

"It's not the same thing." I was getting irritated and frustrated. "I know what I meant. I meant maybe yes and at the same time maybe no."

"I'm sure," Rosemary said.

I could feel myself chipping around the edges. "How about telling what this is all about?"

"They kidnapped her," Charles said.

"That's what we think," Rosemary added.

"Kidnapped her?" I looked from one face to the other. I could see the almost religious belief there.

"Like they did Patty Hearst," Rosemary said.

"Why," her husband said, "it's a classic copy of that case."

The kettle began a rolling boil. I turned off the flame and got down three cups. I kept my back to them while I made the instant coffee.

The nuts, the crazies, the strange ones. I seemed to get all of them. I drew them like a lodestone draws iron filings.

CHAPTER TWO

All right, it looked like I was going to lose an hour or two of sleep. That and I'd have to listen to God knows how much crap in the process. But it was my mistake. I always made that distinction between what I did to myself and what other people did to me. This one belonged about sixty–forty to me.

I placed the coffee on the table and checked the sugar dish before I sat down. "What do the police believe?"

"You've been talking to them?" It was almost an accusation from Charles.

"Listening to you," I said. "And, anyway, what police are we talking about?"

"The one investigating last night's robbery, the one who gave us your name as a witness."

"Ellison," I said.

"He didn't believe us," Rosemary said.

"Tell me about the kidnapping." That was the easy way, agree with them, hear them out and, as soon as I could, get them out the door and lock it behind them.

"That was in late August," Charles said.

"Billie Joe had been accepted at the University of North Carolina at Greensboro."

I nodded. It had been Women's College some years back.

"I was out of town at the time," Charles said. It was given like a fact, but I had a sense that it also meant that he couldn't be blamed. That if he'd been in town, it might not have happened. It might have been a chipping away at his wife. But done carefully so that he could always argue that he hadn't meant it that way at all. It was, he could say, just her defensiveness.

Rosemary told the rest of it. The stores in Kingstree, South Carolina, were fine up to a point. When you really wanted to shop you came to Atlanta. Everybody did. Either that or Charlotte. So she and Billie Joe drove down from Kingstree and they had reservations at the Regency downtown. That was on a Friday. Late that afternoon they'd shopped at Rich's and Davison's. Just the essentials. In some ways the same kinds of things they might have bought in Kingstree, except that there was more choice in Atlanta. The next day, Saturday, they were going to do the real shopping. At Saks Fifth Avenue at Lenox, that sort of place. It was, Rosemary said, important that Billie Joe go off to college with the right clothes.

That night she disappeared.

"How did it happen?" I could see that they didn't like the instant coffee. They were drinking the cognac. Maybe that was because, after a good beginning, the furnace seemed to be putting out cold air. I poured myself another shot and topped off their glasses.

"It was a mistake in judgment," Rosemary said. "I really didn't know how dangerous Atlanta is."

"After an early dinner, Billie Joe said she wanted to see a movie." Charles nodded at the refilled glass, his thanks, and had a small sip.

"I was tired from driving," Rosemary said. "I wanted to rest. Billie Joe promised she'd be careful. She'd take a cab from the hotel to the theater and a cab back. It was early. It should have been safe, even in a city as large as Atlanta."

"What movie was it?" Not that it mattered. Not that I cared. It was time-fill until I could ease them out.

"I don't remember the film but it was showing at the Weis Cinema. That's on ..."

I said I knew where the Weis was. It was near Peachtree and Twelfth, at the far end of what had been the Strip back in the street people days. Now it was a changing area. The build-ing of Colony Square had caused that. And the word was that a number of torches had found work in the area around Tenth Street. People were selling a lot of buildings to the insurance companies.

"The movie should have been over at ten. I waited until eleven before I began to worry. At twelve I called the police."

"And they weren't much help?" That was standard. People expected the police to ride herd on all kids who stayed out late. The law didn't have that kind of manpower.

"They said maybe she'd stopped off for a late snack," Rosemary said.

The phone rang in the bedroom. I said, "Sorry," and left them in the kitchen. On the way through the living room I hit the ther-mostat another lick. The furnace didn't even grunt at me.

Hump said, "Why'd you run off?"

I said I hadn't exactly run off. I'd been made to feel like somebody's old uncle.

"I've moved on," he said. "I'm at this English-pub-type place. Dart boards and Watney's Red Barrel on tap."

"Have one on me."

"No, look, there's a lot of trim here and some of it is in your age bracket."

"I'm busy."

"You mean … with business?"

I said I didn't think so. I told him about the Atkinsons and the part of the story I'd heard about Billie Joe.

"We could use a job," Hump said. That was Hump for you. A couple of lean months and job choice went out with the gar-bage. He was ready for anything that paid real money. And I knew he needed the cash. He threw it around like a drunk pimp sometimes.

I told him I'd wait and see but I didn't think I was much interested in this one. People who killed clerks at 7–11 stores when they didn't have to weren't the kind of people I wanted to know close up.

"Call me in the morning."

I said I would. Late in the morning.

Back in the kitchen I had my look at the Atkinsons. His face was flushed, dark, angry. Hers was ice-white. I had the feeling they'd had an argument while I was on the phone. I gave them time to settle down. I had a sip of cognac and looked at the kitchen clock. It was thirteen minutes of two. Their crippled story, the way it limped, it might be five a.m. before they finished with it.

I leaned back in my chair and nodded at Rosemary Atkinson.

"Finally I went to the police station and I argued with them for a long time. They sent a detective with me and we went to the theater and we rode around the area for more than an hour. We looked in the eating places and we walked through the bars. We didn't find her."

"And the detective said that Billie Joe was probably at the hotel wondering where you were?"

"But she wasn't."

"I flew in the next day," Charles said. "You won't believe how unresponsive the police were."

"I believe," I said.

"It seems that Atlanta is the primary destination for most of the runaways in the Southeast."

"Billie Joe didn't run away." Rosemary was talking to me. I guess she thought she had to convince me. "She was happy. She was looking forward so much to going away to college."

I could figure the rest of it. The police didn't have a body and there wasn't any evidence of a kidnapping and the girl was young and the police decided she was just another runaway. And they'd listed her that way and gone on to other business.

I knew it all. I'd heard it all. I decided I'd do the question-and-answer approach and try to cut down the time it was taking. The his-and-her storytelling would take until breakfast.

"Was there a ransom demand?"

"No," he said.

"Any word from her at all?"

"Nothing."

Rosemary said, "We ran notices in the personal sections of all the local papers."

I knew those too. *Come home, Billie Joe. Mother and father forgive. No questions asked.*

"And we offered a $500 reward for information about her."

"How?"

"On those advertising cards on the insides of Marta buses."

It was a new approach. I didn't ride the buses much but they seemed to advertise everything else. Why not a lost child? "Nothing from that either?"

"Some crank calls," Charles said. "Others seemed promising." He shook his head. "In each case it turned out the person only wanted a chance at the $500 and didn't know a thing about Billie Joe."

"Charles stayed with me for a week."

"I have a business to run," Charles said.

"I know that," she said. Then to me: "I stayed for another week. I spent whole evenings in places like The Lighthouse and the Stein Club. I don't know what they thought of me in places like that."

"At the end of the second week, I told her to come home."

"I didn't want to."

"It was hopeless. I don't know what I really thought. Maybe I began to believe the police. That Billie Joe was a runaway."

"I hated to give up," Rosemary said.

"I convinced her that if Billie Joe wanted to get in touch with us, she knew we'd be in Kingstree."

That took us up to the second week in September. I looked at the clock. We still had the rest of September, October, November and part of December to go. It didn't look promising. The question-and-answer method hadn't worked. Maybe they'd told their story too many times, to the police or to friends. Now it was almost scripted for them: you say this and I say that.

"The robbery last night ... is that the first time you've heard of her? If the girl I saw last night was Billie Joe."

"No," Rosemary said, "there was one other time."

"That was in late October," Charles said.

Two young men and a girl held up a small supermarket off Peachtree Road. There'd been a couple of robberies before that and the owner had put in a security system that included a movie camera that could be activated by the cashier. A detective on robbery detail had a look at the film. He remembered the woman from out of town who'd been raising hell about her daughter being kidnapped. He thought enough of his hunch to check back on the pictures of Billie Joe. He wasn't entirely sure he had a match, but it was close enough so that he'd contacted the Atkinsons in Kingstree.

"I'm sure it was Billie Joe," Rosemary said.

"They weren't very nice about it," Charles said.

That was to be expected. The Atkinsons had been tearing strips of hide off the Atlanta police. Two months of taking that and now the police could say, See, see, see, this daughter you say was kidnapped is a criminal.

"In the film, was she armed?"

"No."

"But the guys were?"

"Both carried guns," Rosemary said.

"Handguns?"

She nodded.

It wasn't a thing most people wanted to believe. The truth: if you pointed a gun at people enough times, sooner or later you pulled the trigger. And most of the time the one with the gun wouldn't be able to say why. Or if there was an answer, it was some kind of Billy the Kid crap. The crazy reasoning: I wanted to see what would happen.

"And if the girl last night was Billie Joe, that's the second job they've pulled?"

"There might be others," Charles said. "The police have four or five more where two young men carried out the actual robberies while someone waited in the car. The police seem to think that Billie Joe might have been the person who remained in the car."

"Well, that's that." I collected the cups and rinsed them and left them in the sink. "I can't say the girl was your daughter and I can't say she wasn't." I tapped the cork into the cognac and looked at them. As far as I was concerned the talk was over. That was it. "I don't mean to be rude but I have to get up early in the morning."

"You're not rude at all," Rosemary said. "You've been kind to listen to us." That wasn't all. I could see that she was looking at her husband. It was his shot.

"Mr. Hardman, I understand you do jobs now and then."

"If you mean P.I. work, I'm not licensed."

"I understand that," Charles said.

"But it's just as well. If I was licensed, this isn't a job I'd take on. It stinks like rotten meat."

"I don't understand you, Mr. Hardman." Her eyes begged at me. "Billie Joe is just a child."

"Then she's not the girl I saw in the 7–11 last night. The girl I saw had just seen a woman killed, maybe a few seconds before, and it didn't seem to bother her at all. Or maybe she pulled the trigger. Whatever. It's a police matter now. Killing is. Robbery is. They'll find your daughter for you . . . if that was your daughter. And if it was, you'd do better to save your money and make a down payment on the best lawyer in the country. Foreman or Bailey, somebody like that."

He accepted it. I'd known he would. That was his businessman's sensibilities. If you accepted the profits, you learned to live with the losses too.

Rosemary said, "But if nobody will help her . . ."

Charles put a hand on her arm and stopped her. I saw a slight shake of his head that silenced her. In the living room he thanked me for the coffee and the brandy while he helped her with her coat. He struggled into his topcoat and waited while I switched on the porch light and opened the door.

"If you change your mind…" she said.

"I won't."

"Rosemary, stop it." It was an order and it was as if he'd hit her between the eyes.

I closed the door and went into the bathroom. I looked at myself in the mirror for a long time. I felt like a number-one bastard. I'd taken worse jobs in my years away from the force. Those favors I did for people with the cash under the table.

I returned to the kitchen and had another shot of the cognac before I put it in the cabinet. The smell of her perfume was in all the rooms. It was gut-grabbing and groin-clawing.

It was an hour or two before I could sleep.

CHAPTER THREE

Of course, I'd lied to the Atkinsons. There wasn't any reason to get up early. I could remain in the blanket womb the rest of the day if I wanted to. It was one of the dull times, days when I thought I needed a hobby like matchbook collecting. Days when I woke up feeling strong and half-convinced myself that I ought to do something about the front yard. By the time I'd had breakfast and read the *Constitution* all that puffed-up energy had vanished. Matchbooks weren't that interesting and the yard could wait another week or two.

Or it could wait until spring.

The dry, burnt taste of cognac outlasted toothpaste and mouthwash. A dull headache reminded me that the brandy had been only six or seven years old. That was raw when you thought of the blends that were fifteen or twenty years in the barrel.

All those cigarettes and that frustrating talk hadn't helped either.

And during the night, almost every hour on the hour, I'd awakened with the nightmarish feeling that the walls and floor of the bedroom were covered with frost. Each time I'd waited for the sound of the furnace cutting in before I dropped back into sleep.

Yes, Jim Hardman has his winter problems.

One more problem rang my doorbell a few minutes before eleven. I opened the door and looked at the young detective who'd been at the 7–11 store a couple of nights before. I remembered that his name was Ellison.

He flipped a cigarette over his shoulder onto my brown winter lawn. "You going to ask me in, Hardman?"

"This business or social?"

"Business," he said.

I backed away. "As long as it's not social."

On the way past me he gave me a slit-eyed stare. "You got something against the police?"

"You don't invite me to your parties anymore."

"If you're not on the list, then there's good reason."

I slammed the door. "So I hear."

He followed me into the kitchen. I got my cup from the table and mixed myself another cup of instant. I returned to the table, sat down and opened the sports page. I'd already read the parts that interested me but he didn't know that.

"You got some coffee you can spare?"

I pointed at the kettle. "Help yourself. Like you said, it's not social."

He selected a cup from the dish rack and rinsed it. He ran a finger around the inside rim of it. That was his way of knocking my lifestyle. I didn't let it bother me. I pretended interest in an article about Georgia Tech basketball.

After he'd made himself some coffee he stood across the table from me. "I figure the Atkinsons stopped by to see you."

"Is that a question?"

There was a beat while he found a spoon and added sugar. "Yes, it's a question."

"They wanted to know if I could identify their daughter as the girl in the store that night."

"Could you?"

"Not really," I said. "Might be and might not be."

"That all?" He gulped the coffee and made a face. "This is awful, you know."

"That's because it's free."

"And that was all of it?"

"As far as I was concerned." I turned the page and creased it carefully. I'd have done the subway fold but I didn't think it would impress him. He was too small town.

"No favors this time, Hardman?"

I kept the paper between us. I tried reading about the Hawks. It was the usual article about their need for a big league center. I'd agreed with the writer the first time he'd written the piece.

"No favors this time?"

"That sounds like a question?"

"No," Ellison said, "that's an order."

"I don't know what you're talking about."

"You know."

I was running out of sports pages. If he stayed much longer, I'd have to read the financial page. While I was thinking about that he solved it for me. He leaned across the table and rammed an open hand down the center of the paper. It tore down the middle and left me holding the corners.

"I'm talking to you."

"No doubt about that." I gathered together the parts of the sports section, wadded it up, and tossed it toward the trash can. It hit the front rim and bounced back. "If I'd hadn't already finished the paper, you'd owe me fifteen cents."

"Try and collect it."

I stood up. I watched him place his cup on the table and straighten up. He was ready. No, that wasn't the way it was going to be. I held it in. I scooped up the ball of newspaper and jammed it into the trash can. "You done, Ellison?"

"For the time." He relaxed.

"The door's not locked."

"I spelled it out for you. No favors. You mix in this and being asshole buddies with Art Maloney won't get you a thing. Not even a half step."

"That's clear enough." I passed him and crossed the living room. I swung the door open and waited.

"I'll see you again," he said on his way out.

"Next time bring a piece of paper that says I've got to talk to you. Be businesslike about it."

He turned on the porch. He had something he wanted to say. I didn't want to hear it. I slammed the door and hit the lock. He shouted. Part of it got lost in the door slam, the rest when I turned and walked back into the kitchen.

It was a dumb move on my part. There were too many ways they could hassle you if they wanted to. Nit-picking shit. Not that it made that much difference with me. They'd already marked me in the black book. Rotten, bad ex-cop. What else could they do to me?

"You should have stayed around last night." Hump slouched in my easy chair. A beer in one hand, a ham sandwich in the other.

"Good trim?"

"An A-minus." If he'd been a cat he'd have purred. *Satisfied* was written on his forehead. "The one I'd picked out for you, she might have been an A-plus."

"I don't like the smell of meat markets."

"Breast of beef, thigh of pig," Hump said.

"Marcy gave me her sorority pin before she left town."

"Morals, morals. Man, you're growing old."

Hump has a lot of trouble with my white cracker ways. It didn't quite even out. I didn't have any trouble understanding his point of view at all. Trim was trim and you didn't pass up any of it. The years you had, that was a one-way trip on a fast train. What you passed up on the first time through you didn't get a second chance at. Wave good-bye at it. Write it off.

In other ways we're alike. Marcy says that we don't have much ambition. That might be true. Might not. Hump is thinking of living long enough to draw his NFL pension. I don't think I'll make it to Social Security.

We do just enough to get by. Jobs and favors that pay cash. Jobs that can't stand sunlight. We like this better than a nine-to-five. Still, income averaging is hard. Some months there's no income at all.

About two in the afternoon I left Hump in the living room with one of the last beers in front of him. I shaved and took a long shower. It was going to be one of those days. A tour of the town. A drink here and a drink there until suppertime. Smashed by seven.

I dressed in shorts and a T-shirt and walked into the living room. I said, "Hey, how about Cognito's for supper tonight?" One look and I backed away and slammed the door behind me. Rosemary Atkinson was seated on the sofa, facing the bedroom. When I did the dinner suggestion, she turned away from Hump and looked at me. I got a quick look at the smile she gave my hairy white legs.

I put on a pair of slacks and some shoes and returned to the living room. By the time I got there, Hump had fixed her a scotch-rocks and I sensed that they were waiting for me.

I noticed one thing right away. She looked younger. The night before I'd placed her age close to that of her husband. Today she looked ten years younger and that was probably the right year count. She dressed it too. She was wearing a pair of those recycled jeans sewn out of patches and squares, a black wool turtleneck and black kid boots. What looked like a thigh-length suede coat was at one end of the sofa.

The matter of age brought up an interesting possibility: was the way she looked the night before a concession to her husband? Was it a pretense that she was forty-five and only looked thirty-five?

"Mr. Evans seemed interested in my story about Billie Joe."

"He's got a big heart," I said.

"At least a heart," she said.

I shrugged and went into the kitchen. I looked into the refrigerator and saw that Hump had made another trip while I was showering. No beer. I got a couple of ice cubes, added a splash of scotch and a trickle of water and stirred it with a finger. I leaned in the doorway and looked at them.

"You remember the detective you talked to … Ellison?"

She nodded.

"He was my first visitor of the day. He told me, in no uncertain terms, to stay out of this."

"Can he do that?"

"That's not the question. What he can do is make my life miserable."

"You never let that crap bother you before," Hump said.

"That's true." I rounded the coffee table and sat on the sofa next to the suede coat. "This time I'm not sure it's worth bucking it."

"Go ahead and say it," Rosemary said.

"Say what?"

"What's really bothering you."

"You got here a day late. You missed the body behind the counter. Maybe you ought to make a trip to the morgue. There's a thirty-one-year-old woman over there. Somebody shot her a couple of times. I was there before the police. I didn't see a gun in the place. I don't think she was armed, so I don't know why they shot her. And I bet they don't even know why they shot her."

"Give the rest of the lecture," Hump said.

"Is it that obvious?" I nodded and shook out a smoke. I lit it and looked at Rosemary. "I don't know what's happening anymore. It's like life's not worth much. You know the take from that 7-11 robbery? Might have been three hundred dollars. How do you stack that against a life? Ain't no way I know. But one of those kids or two of them—at least two rounds were fired—decided their need for money was more important than that woman's life. That's a shitty decision. It puts me on the other side of the fence from them. If I got involved in this, I'd be the hunter with a gun. I'd be saying stop the same time I was pulling trigger."

"Then you'd be as bad as you say they are," Rosemary said.

"Maybe. I don't think so."

Hump wagged a couple of fingers at me. I tossed him the pack of Pall Malls. "And if the girl is being coerced, Jim?"

"You believe that?"

He nodded toward Rosemary. "She believes it."

"And all mothers believe their daughters are virgins."

He lit a smoke and blew it toward the ceiling. "You're rough today."

That was a fair estimate. I couldn't argue with him. I liked to think I had some balance. That I could look at most things straight on. Now I was out of sync. I had, since the night in the 7–11, what amounted to a permanent tilt. I wasn't looking at the same world everybody else saw.

"Charles drove back to Kingstree this morning," Rosemary said. "I stayed behind. I hope there's something I can do. And I thought you might reconsider."

"Why me? You act like I'm the only one in town. There's probably a whole yellow page of P.I.'s. One of them would be glad to take this on."

"You've seen her," she said.

"That's not enough."

"It is for me."

I shook my head. "Count me out." I got up and carried my drink into the bedroom. I closed the door behind me. I found a clean shirt in the dresser and tore the wrappings away. I was putting it on when Hump came in.

"You're wrong about this, Jim."

"You ask her what happens if you find the girl?"

"No."

"You ought to," I said.

"What does that mean?"

"It's about what money buys. It'll buy you too and if you find that girl and she turns out to be Billie Joe, she'll be back over the South Carolina border so fast you won't believe it. And no matter what the truth is, they'll buy a fancy lawyer and a fancy psychiatrist and they'll say, yes, this poor little rich girl took part in those robberies but she was forced to do it. They brainwashed her; they threatened her."

"What the hell do you want, Jim?"

I stuffed the shirttail in and fumbled with the buttons. We were about as close to a fight as we'd ever been in the years we'd been together, during the time we'd had our loose partnership. I took my time. I had a sip of the scotch. "All right, I want this much. People who believe in the law keep talking about everybody deserving their day in court. I don't think that just means the living. It means the dead as well. That thirty-one-year-old woman deserves justice as much as that pretty blond daughter. Maybe more because everybody seems to be forgetting about her."

"And if Billie Joe was coerced?"

"Prove it in court."

"I believe that's what she intends," Hump said.

"Want a bet on that?"

He shook his head. "I don't bet with close-in people."

It was as close as he could come to saying friends.

"I'm going to help her if I can, Jim."

"I figured as much."

"Hard feelings?"

"Not a one." I tapped him on the shoulder as he stepped away.

Five minutes later, when I returned to the living room, it was empty. They'd left.

I ran small circles in big circles all afternoon. I had a couple of late afternoon drinks at the 1776 on Luckie. Then I walked the two blocks to the Carnegie Way Library and read a couple of picture books on old firearms. Now that was a hobby that grabbed me more than matchbooks.

At six-thirty, I called Hump's apartment from the pay phone in the library basement. There was a chance he'd still like to have dinner. There wasn't any answer.

Around seven, I stopped at the Kroger's at Ansley Mall and picked out a steak. At the nearby wine shop I bought a case of Bud and a bottle of a Beaujolais Villages.

I cooked the steak in my old cast-iron skillet and drank the whole bottle of wine with it. At ten-thirty, I wobbled off to bed.

I don't know how long the phone had been ringing. As far under as I was, it could have been ten minutes or longer. I fumbled a hand across the table top until I found the phone.

"Jim?"

"Yeah?"

"This is Hump. I'm in a bind."

With my free hand I continued to search the table top, looking for my watch. It was a few seconds before I realized it was still on my wrist. That was the wine. By the luminous dial it was six minutes after midnight. "Where are you?"

"At the Majestic eating pork chops and eggs."

That was the all-night diner near the Plaza Drugs. "What's the problem?"

"I've got a bunch of bikers after my ass."

"That never bothered you before," I said.

"One or two might not," he said. "This is more like a dozen."

"Fifteen minutes," I said. "Sit tight. Don't leave."

"I ain't about to. They're outside."

He broke the connection. I dressed and got the .38 P.P. from the shoebox in my closet. Maybe I'd need it. Maybe not. I hoped not.

CHAPTER FOUR

I turned off North Highland directly into a parking spot in front of the Plaza Drugs. From my car, turning and looking through the rear side window, I could see the front entrance of the Majestic Cafe. The door faced the far end of the large parking lot. Of the string of stores and shops that formed an "L," only the Plaza and the Majestic were lit up at this hour.

I didn't have any trouble finding the bikers. Two of them stood, mock casual, in the greenish neon light that flooded the sidewalk. The others hadn't hidden either. At the last parking space, the one nearest the Cafe and fronting on Ponce de Leon, there was a swarm of them. I didn't do a head count but I saw seven or eight of them standing and leaning around an old blue VW van. All of the bikers wore the uniform—leather jackets, boots and jean pants.

They had Hump in a box, just waiting for him to finish his pork chops and eggs and walk into the middle of it. I got out of my Ford and dug in my pocket for change. No dime. I went in the Plaza Drugs and bought a pack of smokes. I made certain I got a dime in the change.

"Pay phone?"

The dull-eyed lady cashier nodded toward the door. "Outside."

I found the phone booth and dialed the police department number from memory. As soon as the switchboard answered I said, "I'm Ashley Phillips of 967 North Highland. I want to report some trouble."

"Tell me about it."

"I just left the Majestic Cafe, the one near the Plaza Drugs."

"Yes."

"A whole bunch of those bikers are outside. Two of them, on the walk, pushed me and said they were going to kick somebody's butt and it might as well be mine. And there's about eight or ten more standing by a van."

"They pushed you?"

"Almost knocked me down. And those bikers and the others are shouting back and forth at each other like they're about to start a fight or something."

"Where are you now?"

"I'm at the phone booth near the drugstore."

"You stay there and when the police arrive you tell them who you are. They'll need your full story."

I said that I certainly would, that I was a good citizen, and I hung up and walked back to my car. I got in long enough to take the .38 out of my waistband and stash it away in the glove compartment. It wouldn't do to be found carrying. With police on the way I didn't think I'd need it.

I headed for the Majestic. I did a wide loop that kept me away from the van where the large group of bikers was. Even at that distance I could smell grass on the cold wind that blew toward me. Past the van I angled toward the Cafe door. When I reached the walk the two bikers gave me a slow, long look. One turned away and I read the back of his leather jacket. *Atlanta Outlanders.* Below that was a design that was either the widespread horns of some long-horn bull or the handles of a hog bike. Perhaps it was supposed to suggest both.

It wasn't a biker outfit I'd heard about. Still, there was a lot of shifting around going on. One bunch of them coming to town and another leaving. The police hassled them when they could and that probably accounted for the departures. A couple of months back there'd been a big trial. A biker from another bunch had raped a girl while his buddies were beating up her boyfriend. Just before the trial, two of the accused bikers had tried to kill the girl to keep her from testifying. They'd blinded her in one eye and torn up her face with a shotgun blast in a high-speed chase on the highway. That incident fresh in their minds and the way the police felt about bikers anyway, that was what I was counting on.

I stopped near the cash register and looked down the counter. Hump was seated, head down, at a stool at the back. There was an empty seat on the other side of him. He didn't look up when I sat down next to him. He had a pork chop bone in one hand, gnawing at it.

"See them?"

"They're hard not to see."

"What's your count?" He cropped the bone on his plate and wiped his hands with a napkin.

"Too many."

A waitress stopped in front of me. I ordered coffee.

"We going to camp here all night?"

I shook my head. "I'd say maybe five minutes more."

"Huh?"

"Wait and see."

My coffee came. I sipped at it. A couple of swallows and I turned on the stool and looked outside. I checked my watch. It was about time. And there wasn't any doubt the cops would come. They wouldn't miss a chance to hassle the bikers. It was one of their late-night sports.

I'd expected sirens. They didn't come that way. I think they didn't want to flush them. What I heard first was the squeal of tires and the slamming of car doors. It was loud enough so that heads turned in the Cafe. Two floor waitresses ran to the door and looked out.

"I said, "Now, Hump."

I grabbed my check. He grabbed his. By the time we reached the cash register, the aisle was packed with people who were pushing and shoving to get a view of what was going on outside. I found change to cover my tab and dropped it on the counter. Hump fumbled with some bills and placed the checks and the bills next to mine. I followed in Hump's wake as he spread the people. We reached the walk.

There were five squad cars out front. Two were on the Ponce de Leon side of the Cafe. Three others, at odd angles, blocked the VW van.

The two bikers who'd been watching the front of the Majestic were spread, leaning forward, hands on the wall. Two uniformed cops backed them. Another uniformed cop stood a couple of paces away. He held a length of heavy chain in one hand, a length of heavy pipe in the other.

One of the spread bikers turned his head and saw Hump. He said, "Hey, you…" and tried to push himself away from the wall. The cop behind him didn't say anything. He stepped back about half a pace and hit the biker on the point of his shoulder with a billy. I don't know if it broke anything. The biker's knees gave under him and his face hit the wall. The cop backing the other biker stepped forward and hit the downed biker across the back with his billy. The *whomp* had the sound of somebody kicking a football.

I caught Hump at the elbow and pushed him toward a wide circle away from the van. "My car," he said.

"Later," I said. "I'm by the drugstore."

I got behind the wheel. Hump slid into the passenger seat. I turned and looked back toward the Majestic. It was getting rough around the van. Voices were rising and the shouting had "motherfucker" and "scumbag" laced in it. It looked like the ass-kicking and head-busting was about to begin. I'd seen all that before.

I backed out, turned onto North Highland, and headed home.

❧   ❧   ❧

I couldn't keep my eyes open. I ran cold water into the washbasin and dunked my face in it. I returned to the kitchen and found that Hump had made a couple of cups of coffee. I leaned over the cup and blinked into the steam. I was still shivering from the cold drive. And now, for some reason, the furnace was putting out more heat than it had for months.

"At this rate," I said, "you're never going to get that gold-plated Junior G-Man badge."

"What's that supposed to mean?"

"Your first job and you get run to ground by some bikers who want to beat on you with chains and pipes."

"And that wasn't the half of it," he said.

"What did the bikers have against you?"

"All I did was ask some questions."

"The right ones or the wrong ones?"

"Must have been the wrong ones for them," he said.

"Start from the beginning."

"At six, I dropped Rosemary at her hotel."

Six? I did some simple math. There were three hours or so missing in there somewhere. "Is that the beginning?"

"We talked some at my place. There was a lot I didn't know. In fact, if you hadn't been so short with her, there were some things she'd have told you that she couldn't in front of her husband."

I sipped the coffee. "Such as?"

"The daughter, Billie Joe, is illegitimate."

"And her husband doesn't know?"

"He knows all right. That's one of the problems. He's been hard on the girl. Too hard. It's like he thinks she'll make the same mistakes her mother did. Hell, he wouldn't let her date until last year. Her senior year in high school."

"Why's that important?"

"It set up the big lie," Hump said.

"Which was?"

"The night Billie Joe disappeared she didn't go to a movie by herself. She went off to meet a boy she knew. He'd been in high school with her, a year ahead of her, and he'd come to Atlanta to go to college."

"Tech?"

"Georgia State. The way Rosemary remembers it, the boy moved to Atlanta and got a job and was going to school at night."

"And the kidnapping, all that crap, was to cover up the fact that Rosemary hadn't played the tough mama the way she was supposed to?"

"Rosemary is scared to death of her husband ... whatever his name is."

"Charles," I said.

"The lie was in the beginning. It was the only explanation she could give her husband. Later, when Billie Joe didn't come back, she began to believe it. Really believe it."

I closed my eyes and rubbed at them. "Go on with it. You dropped Rosemary at her hotel around six."

It was going on seven by the time Hump found a parking space near Georgia State. It's one of those inner-city schools. No campus as such and no dorms. There's an extensive building program underway but downtown property is so valuable in Atlanta that there are no frills. There's a postage stamp park with some shrubs and flowers and a fountain near the Ad building. The rest of the college is composed of buildings that look like fairly ordinary office space.

It took some asking before Hump found the Evening College office. Maybe it was early or supper-time. The office was empty except for a young black girl. Not prime, Hump thought, but not a cull either. He leaned on the counter and waited for her to notice him.

Kind of bowlegged. He watched her walk toward him. Thighs like a mare. And her eyes aware of how closely he watched her. She stopped a step away from the counter. "Can I help you?"

"I need a transcript."

"Your transcript?"

"No, it's for a boy wants to work for me. His name's Carl Culp." Hump dug out his roll of cash. "I understand there's a charge for a copy."

"Copies are made by the day staff," the girl said. She lifted a pad from under the counter and poised a pen over it. "If you'll give me your name and your business address…"

"Hump Evans." He watched her mouth fall open. "But, look, this is a rush. I can't wait long for a copy. I've got to make a decision in the next day or two."

"*The* Hump Evans?" A smile, a bird-catching and -eating smile.

"I'm the only one I know."

"Then you know my cousin, Emma Jane Green. She works for the phone company."

He did. Emma Jane was the fat girl that Hardman said looked like a busted bale of hay. "Sure. She's a nice girl."

"She speaks highly of you too." Sly knowledge in her face. Looks like those girls have kissed and told. "Why, she talks about you all the time."

"I don't know what she'd have to talk about." Sly right back at her.

"Emma Jane might be exaggerating some."

"It's according to what she said."

"I don't think I could repeat it," the girl said. "Not until I knew you well enough."

"That's easy," Hump said. "We can have a drink one night and, after you know me better, we could check it out against the truth."

A wide smile. "How would we do that checking?"

"We'd find a way."

Her pen moved over the pad. She tore the top sheet away and pushed it toward him. Her name was there and the office number. Sarah Barker. "I'm through here at ten."

"Ten's a good time. But first I've got this problem."

"The transcript? I'd like to help you, but they've got these definite rules about ..."

"For all I know," Hump said, "that boy might not have gone to this school at all. He might have made it up."

"Maybe I can do that much for you. What's his name?"

"Carl Culp."

She took a step away before she looked over her shoulder at him. "Now, don't you go away."

Hump grinned and shook his head. Oh, yes. Sparks and dark fire, oh, yes.

A walk like a dance step when she returned from a room down a hallway. Let him have a good look at it. Bowed legs are pretty because my mama said they were. She winked as she placed a gray folder on the counter and lifted the cover. "He took six courses here."

"Just six?" Hump put out a hand and turned the folder toward him. "That's one lie. He told me more than that."

"You're not supposed to ..."

"A peek won't hurt." He gave her his high-voltage grin. "In fact, sometimes a peek is a lot of fun."

A breathy whisper: "Well, if you hurry. Doctor Bracy ought to be back any minute."

Four Cs, one D and an Incomplete. "His grades suck."

"That might be why he's not in school this term."

"Might be."

While his finger traced the grades, his eyes were searching the top of the page. He wanted a street address. He found it, an address on Argonne, and repeated it to himself a time or two.

She was worried. "Doctor Bracy'll be . . ."

He closed the folder and pushed it across the counter toward her. "I think I saved myself a dollar or two. It might be the cost of a drink."

"My drink's scotch."

"That makes you my twin," Hump said. "J&B?"

"That's a good one."

"And you're off at ten?"

"On the dot," she said.

Hump backed away. "I'll call you."

"You won't forget?"

Hump laughed. "Me forget Emma Jane Green's cousin?" He waved and backed through the doorway.

"This Carl Culp, he's the boy that Billie Joe was supposed to meet that night?" I got the open bottle of cognac from the cabinet. The coffee had cooled enough so that the alcohol wouldn't steam away. I poured in cognac until the mixture reached the rim of the cup. I pushed the bottle toward Hump.

He nodded. "The old high school friend."

"And this Culp turned out to be a biker?"

Hump laughed at me. "You said you wanted it from the beginning. You want me to leave out the middle?"

"Tell it your way," I said.

It was cruising time in that part of town when Hump got there. Even in cold weather the young men lounged on the corners. Usually they were near bus stops in case the cops happened by. They could always say they were waiting for the 45 bus. These were the money-trade walkers. The others, the ones with cars, waited until later and leapfrogged their cars along the stretch of road near the lake in Piedmont Park.

Driving slow, trying to catch one number so he'd know where he was, Hump passed the bus stop at Fifth and Argonne. A blond young man dressed in jeans and a fringed leather jacket leaned on the bus stop post and waved at him. There was enough light so that Hump could see that the kid had stuffed his jock with a T-shirt or a length of garden hose.

Down another block and he found the house. It had been painted with what must have been government surplus paint. A lead-like battleship gray. In the wind, on the porch, he burned a book of matches reading the name cards on the bank of mailboxes.

No Carl Culp. He tried the door that led to the downstairs hallway. It was unlocked. There were three apartments on the first floor. He banged on two doors before he found someone at home.

A young, dark-haired girl kept the chain on and squinted at him. The ammonia-strong scent of a cat-box drifted past her and hit Hump in the face. It brought tears to his eyes. "I'm looking for Carl Culp."

"I don't know him."

"You know anybody who might ...?"

"The resident manager."

"Where does he live?"

"Apartment number one at the foot of the stairs."

She closed the door. Hump went to the outside door and opened it. He took a few deep breaths and his eyes cleared. When he felt better he returned to the apartment at the foot of the stairs. He didn't bother to knock. A notepad was thumbtacked to the door. A message was scrawled on it. *Back at 9.*

It was time for supper anyway. He got in his Buick and turned around in a driveway and headed for Fifth and Argonne. As he turned left on Fifth his headlight swept across the bus stop there. The young blond boy was leaning on the window of a white Mercedes sedan. Hump couldn't see the man inside but he thought he got a flash of gray hair.

"And that young boy was Carl Culp?" I had finished the coffee. I rinsed out the cup and poured some straight cognac in it.

"Of course not," Hump said.

"You're making a lot of him."

"That's just setting the area for you," he said.

"I know the area."

"You been cruising there, Jim?"

"Not as recently as you have," I said.

He gave it up and went on with his story.

He had supper at Brothers Two at Colony Square. It was a longer supper than he'd intended. There was a black girl, an actress who worked in TV commercials, at the bar and he'd asked her to have the meal with him. After all he was working and he had an advance from Rosemary Atkinson. So he'd taken his time over the prime rib and he had talked some candy nonsense to the girl and it had been almost ten before he left. He'd promised to drop by Harrison's later and look for the girl if he got done with the job by then.

"You're insatiable," I said.

"Huh?" Hump blinked at me.

"First the Atkinson woman and then ..."

"I didn't put a glove on her," Hump said.

"Who does it with gloves on?"

"That's it. Now I've got it. That's what's been bothering you. You're jealous. That Rosemary got to you."

"Bullshit."

"And I knew it the whole time. That's why I didn't put a glove on her. I've been saving her for you." He tipped back his cup and big-eyed me over the rim. "And the truth is I felt, the way she acted, that she had the itch for you too."

"Game-playing," I said. "You know that's shit."

"I've got the hotel where she's staying and her room number. I did it all for you, buddy."

"Go on with the story."

Phil Grant was the resident manager. Bald on top with long stringy hair that touched the collar of his unbuttoned tie shirt. A T-shirt under that with tomato or catsup stains on it. He clutched a paperback edition of Hart Crane's poetry, a finger inserted in it to mark his place.

"He moved out a couple of months ago."

"He leave a forwarding address?"

"Not with me. He might have filled out one of those cards at the post office."

"Could be." Hump nodded his thanks and stepped away. He turned back to Grant as he was about to close the door. "Look, maybe you know where he works."

"I know where he used to work."

"That might help," Hump said.

"Out past Brookwood Station. You know where that is?"

Hump nodded.

"First gas station on the left past Brookwood."

"I know it."

"He was pumping gas there the last time I saw him."

Making the turn from Argonne onto Fifth Street, Hump saw that the blond stud in denim had been replaced by another one who wore black leather and a white stocking cap.

It was brief and to the point. The owner, a dumpy man in khakis and a Braves ball cap, said, "I had to fire him. It wasn't that he didn't do good work. He was a good worker but he was hanging around with a biker gang. I started missing some gas. It wasn't much. A few gallons at first. You see, the meter reading and the gas sales key on the register weren't matching up. That went on too long. So I sat across the street in my car a couple of nights. One night six bikers came up and Carl gassed them and they rode off without paying. That's twenty-five or thirty gallons right there. And that was that, the way I felt."

"Know which biker gang it was?"

"Atlanta Outlanders," the dumpy man said.

"I didn't know what else to do," Hump said. "So I did the Hardman fallback."

"What's that?"

"It could be a new dance step but it ain't. It means when you need to know something you call a friendly cop."

"Hardman fallback? I like that."

"I thought you would," Hump said. "It's like having a mountain named after you."

Art Maloney called back in ten minutes. "I was right about it. Bill Dexter in Intelligence has been keeping tabs on them. All the biker gangs. There was a big convention, or whatever they call it, here in town a few months back. Gangs from all over. There was a bit of trouble. Not as much as they expected but enough so that the Department decided to put a man on them part time."

"He know the Outlanders?"

"It's one of the new ones. A splinter off another gang. Dexter was at home and he doesn't have his notes with him. In fact, he sounded like he'd had a few drinks. Couldn't seem to remember much. Just enough. You know Greenwood, that circle that runs between Monroe and Charles Allen?"

Hump said he did.

"About halfway down the circle, on the left, there's an old white frame house. It's got a chain-link fence around the front yard. Usually there's a bike or two in the yard. That's where the Outlanders live. Or did."

"Thanks, Art."

"Where's Hardman?"

"At home sucking his thumb."

"You told him that?"

"It was the truth." Hump drew the cognac bottle toward him and tipped it and poured a big shot in his coffee cup. "I didn't explain it. I didn't say it was over some married woman you'd just met."

"Nice of you," I said.

"I thought so too. I couldn't think of any reason why Art ought to know your business."

Even in the cold wind, the wind whipping down the street, the front yard smelled like a grease pit at a service station. Three "hogs" with the high chrome handlebars were parked in the right half of the rutted and almost grassless front yard.

The windows were covered. Some light leaked from the sides. From the steps, Hump could hear hard rock played at some window-shaking and eardrum-breaking level. The porch creaked under his weight. He stopped. He needed some time to come up with a scam, some way of explaining why he'd dropped by. He'd tried two or three and discarded them when time ran out. He heard a chain rattle off to his right, at the far end of the porch.

"Who's that?"

"Hump Evans."

"What you want?" Clump of heavy boots as the man moved from the darkness.

"I'm visiting," Hump said.

"No way," the man said. "This place is posted."

The man moved into the spill of light. He was big, six-two or so, and dressed all in leather. Black leather jacket and pants. He was white and his red hair was elaborately frizzled and curled. The chain rattled. The man carried about a five-foot length of chain. It was doubled over, the ends gripped in the man's right hand. "Move on, boy."

"I need to see somebody."

"You're seeing somebody," the red-haired man said.

"Carl Culp."

"He ain't here. Try lighting a candle for him."

"You saying he's dead?"

"I didn't say that." The chain rattled. "Now get your ass off my porch."

"Not right away. First I want to find out where Carl …"

Hump saw the man shove his left leg forward and plant it. The chain whipped back. Hump spoiled it by stepping in close. His right shoulder hit the man and threw him off balance. His left hand fumbled, caught the man's right elbow, and slipped down until he gripped the wrist. He put all the pressure on the wrist that he could. The man was strong. He didn't release the chain.

It was a standoff. The red-haired man tried a kick with his heavy boots. Hump felt the shift in weight and slipped the kick. When the foot drew back, Hump stepped on it and ground it down. The man yelled. "Shorty. Shorty."

The front door opened. Light flooded the part of the porch where Hump was. He turned his head and looked.

A short, blocky man with black hair stood there. He wore jeans and a blue T-shirt. In one hand he held a .45 automatic. "What's this shit?"

"This spade is looking for Culp."

The short man curled his thumb upward and pulled back the hammer of the .45. "Step away or I'll put a hole in you."

Hump shoved the red-haired man away and turned. He looked into the eye of the .45. "This hassle ain't necessary. All I want to know is how I can get in touch with Carl Culp."

The red-haired man behind him hit him across the back of the neck with the length of chain. He didn't go out but he fell to his knees. While he was on all fours the short man pushed away from the doorway and kicked him in the chest.

CHAPTER FIVE

touched the back of his neck. Hump winced and pushed my hand away. There were lumpy welts and the skin wasn't broken. "How does it feel?"

"It's going to be a sore mother tomorrow," he said.

"Maybe we can hold the swelling down." I got a plastic bag from the cabinet under the sink and filled it with ice cubes. I pressed it against the back of Hump's neck and held it there until he reached back and caught it. "How's your chest?"

"I don't think anything is broken. I've been counting ribs the last hour or so and I don't seem to have any extra ones."

I sat down across the table from him. "So you were under the gun?"

"And on the floor," Hump said.

He felt himself being dragged into the house. In the front room, the living room, there was the smell of hashish. The burnt-wood-chip smell. The one with the .45, Shorty, stepped away from Hump and said, "Watch him, Curly."

Hump was on hands and knees. He watched Shorty move to the tape machine and cut the volume down. There was jerky movement at the sofa. A brown-haired girl with a wisp of blond pubic hair sat up and jumped away from the sofa. In her nakedness he could see the abuse she'd been taking. Bruises and dark places on her thin body and a tailpipe burn on the inside of her right leg.

Her face twisted. She shrieked, "Shorty, I said I'd do anything you said but I ain't going to do no nigger."

"Go in the other room, Sally."

This nigger wouldn't touch you, Hump thought. He watched the child's body as she turned away. The bony pelvis, the small breasts like eggs. Sixteen and already rank spoiled.

A wooden cable reel served as a table in front of the sofa. Shorty sat down on the sofa and placed the .45 on the reel. He lifted a brass hash pipe. He lit the hash with a kitchen match and drew in a deep swallow.

"I'm standing up," Hump said. "Nothing sudden."

Shorty nodded, holding the smoke in.

Hump got to his feet. He felt himself swaying, knees weak and head fogged. "Better," he said, but he didn't believe it.

The hash hissed in the pipe bowl. "What is it you want, man?" Shorty asked.

"I'm looking for Carl Culp." Hump nodded toward Curly and felt his neck stiffening. "This one before it got rough, said something that sounds like he might be dead."

"Might be dead?" Shorty mocked Hump. "Well, if he is I don't know about it."

"That was a put-on," Curly said.

Hump pointed at the hash pipe. "I take a hit?"

"An upright type like you?"

"Might be good for my hurts," Hump said.

Shorty moved the pipe to the side of the table near Hump. He picked up the .45 and leaned back. "Help yourself."

Hump balanced the wood ball tip in his mouth and picked up a match. He held the flame over the bowl and drew in. The pipe load was about done but there was enough for one more hit. Hump held the smoke in his lungs and placed the pipe on the table. When he could talk once more he said, "Appreciate it."

Curly grunted. "The nigger appreciates it."

"Good shit." Hump could feel the first part of it, the first tingle. "Look, I didn't mean to break in on your party."

"Which party?" Shorty grinned. "Poker in the kitchen or balling in the bedroom?"

"Either," Hump said.

"You walked into it," Shorty said. "The question is whether you'll ever walk out of it."

Curly, on Hump's left, shifted his feet. "What's your interest in Culp?"

"Not much. A friend from his hometown, that's Kingstree, asked me to look him up."

"That's the town all right. So why're you looking here?"

"Word is he was hanging around with you."

"Sucking up is more like it," Shorty said.

"He wasn't a member?"

"Him?" Shorty slapped the butt of the .45 against his thigh. "On his best day he couldn't wash my dirty underwear. All he was good for was a free tank of gas now and then."

"When's the last time you saw him?"

"He just drifted off," Curly looked at Shorty. "Back in November, wasn't it?"

"About that."

"Where was he living then?"

"Somewhere on Argonne, I think." Curly looked at the chain in his hand. He wrapped it around his waist, looped it and drew it tight. "I never saw the place."

"You ever see him with a girl? A blond about eighteen, pretty? Her name's Billie Joe. That would have been in late August or September."

"Him with a girl?" Shorty waved a hand toward the bedroom where the thin girl had gone. "When we let him, he got leftovers."

"Low pig in the house," Curly said.

"Acourse, we didn't know him until the middle of September," Shorty said. "Right?"

"One hundred percent," Curly said.

Shorty pulled the hash pipe toward him. He placed the .45 on the table and reached in the pocket of his jeans. He brought out something wrapped in tinfoil. He unwrapped it and it looked like a square of bittersweet chocolate. He broke off a corner chip and placed it in the pipe. "What comes to me is that you aren't really asking about Culp. You're asking about the girl."

"Might sound that way," Hump said.

Shorty struck a kitchen match on the table top and held the flame over the chip. He took a deep puff.

It was the right time. Hump said, "Who killed Carl Culp?"

Shorty choked on the hash smoke. To Hump's left, Curly fumbled with the chain. He was unlooping it when Hump turned and hit him with a right in the mouth. Curly grabbed at his teeth and fell backward. Across the cable-reel table Shorty was still coughing. He slammed the pipe down and grabbed for the .45.

Hump kicked out and caught the table edge with the sole and heel of one shoe. It tilted the table. The movement displaced the .45. Shorty's hand hit nothing but table top. He said, "Goddamn," and fumbled for it. Hump reached across the table and caught the .45 at the same moment Shorty did. He pressed the .45 to the table with his left hand. Shorty tried to jerk it away. That didn't work. He wasn't as strong as Curly. So he leaned away and hit Hump with a left. Hump saw the fist coming and slid under it. It scraped his right ear and burned.

Hump hit Shorty with a short right and stretched him out. Hump had the .45. He ejected the clip and shoved that in his coat pocket. He whirled and threw the .45 into the far corner of the room. The .45 bounced off the wall. It made a racket. A fat girl with black hair, wearing nothing but a T-shirt, ran out of the bedroom and stood staring at him. The skin of her lower body and legs looked like curdled milk. After a moment of shock, the girl put back her head and screamed.

A man with a husky voice said, "What the fuck, Red?"

Hump ran out the front door. He was across the street, getting into his Buick, when the front door opened and about eight or ten bikers, some dressed and others dressing, ran onto the porch. They were yelling and shouting.

All down the street the lights went out.

Hump dropped the clip on the kitchen table. I picked it up and checked it. It was a part load, only four rounds showing. I slid the clip back to him. "Might have been one in the chamber."

"Maybe they didn't know it."

"To find out, all they had to do was point it."

He shrugged. "I guess I lose a couple of points for that." He had a swallow of the cognac. "But don't I get points for getting away?" He took the plastic bag of ice cubes from his neck and looked at it. "You sure this does any good?"

I shook my head. Hump tossed the bag into the sink. Cups and dishes rattled.

"And they followed you?"

"In that blue van. On my tail the whole way. Over to Charles Allen, a left on Ponce de Leon, all the way to the Plaza. I thought about driving over here but I didn't think it was a good idea."

I could see the two of us against about ten of them. It wasn't a good picture in my head.

"I decided it was better where there were some other people."

"And a telephone," I said.

"That too."

I drained the last of the cognac from my cup. I carried it to the sink and rinsed it. "You can have the sofa it you want it."

"Since I don't have wheels that might be a good idea."

"We'll get it first thing in the morning."

He trailed me into the living room. I moved the coffee table. He worked at the sofa until it opened into a bed. While he did that I got him sheets, a pillow and a blanket. I tossed them to him and he sat down and held them across his knees.

"My first time out, how'd I do, boss?" The *boss* was sarcastic. "Is that a B or a C?"

"You're still alive," I said. "I never give the final grades with a headful of wine and brandy." I stopped in the bedroom door.

"I'm seeing Rosemary in the morning."

"That ought to be fun," I said.

"That's not what I meant. I meant I'd appreciate it if you'd talk to her with me."

"I'll sleep on it."

"Sleep?"

"Dream."

I did dream. There I was running through fields of flowers, reds and blues and yellows. I was with Rosemary. I was younger in that dream, about thirty, and she looked about eighteen. It was Rosemary. I knew that. But there was something of the girl in the 7–11 store in her as well.

The dream had the texture, the feeling of a scene out of *Wild Strawberries*.

After the dream went on for a time I realized that we weren't alone. A little blond girl, four or five years old, was running in the field with us. She was holding on to her mother's flowing white dress. Every time I got close to Rosemary, I tripped over the little girl.

That was the dream. I don't remember much more of it. If there was anymore.

I awoke about seven, still tired. I guess it was all that running.

I had my breakfast and waited for Hump to roll himself off the sofa. I rattled enough pots and pans to wake up an army barracks. It worked after a time. He showered and came into the kitchen, rubbing a stiff neck. He ate about everything left in the refrigerator and did it the hard way: the "square meal" style out of one of those old West Point movies. His chest hurt and he couldn't lean forward and he couldn't move his neck. At a kind of attention, he had to lift that fork quite a distance.

"Those two dudes just about ruined me," he said.

"Or the ice pack did. I can't remember whether you're supposed to use ice or heat." I mixed him a second cup of coffee and watched him slosh it about.

"I may have to look those boys up one day."

"Somebody might do it for you," I said.

"You?"

I laughed and shook my head. "I've been thinking about what Curly said to you. About lighting a candle for Carl Culp. You think he meant it?"

"He was a smartass," Hump said, "but it came out funny, odd."

"If what he meant was that Culp wasn't around, that he didn't know where Culp was, why put the death mark on it?"

"Beyond me."

I waited until he wiped the last smear of egg from his plate with a corner of toast. I dropped the plate in the sink and headed for the bedroom. "What was that new dance step you named after me?"

"The Jim Hardman fallback?"

"That's the one and I'm proud of it." I placed my cup on the night table by the bed and dialed the police department number. I got switched to Art Maloney's extension.

"I've got my topcoat on," Art said.

"I've got a name for you and a question."

Hump came in and stood next to the bed, listening.

"I haven't got time," Art said. "I'm due home. Edna's got breakfast started."

"It's worth a bottle of booze. You name the brand."

"I've got a taste for that cognac you had last winter, the good stuff in the green bottle."

That was the sixteen- or seventeen-year-old stuff. It sold for about thirty dollars, give or take a dollar or two. "A deal."

"Payable when?"

"Later today."

"All right. I just took off my topcoat."

"His name is Carl Culp. He'd be somewhere around twenty. Last address over on Argonne. He was working at jobs and going to night school at Georgia State."

"That rings a bell pretty far off. What exactly did this…?"

"You got a body fits that?"

"The bell's closer in. I'll call you back."

I broke the connection and stood up. Hump moved around me and eased himself to a seat on the edge of the bed. "You got a phone book?"

"Under the bed."

He leaned forward and caught himself. Pain track-walked across his face. I got the book for him and blew the dust cotton candy away. "The Riviera," Hump said.

I found the phone number and read it to him so that he could dial. I dropped the phone book on the floor and nudged it under the bed with a toe. I headed for the kitchen. I reached the door about the time he got the call through.

"Rosemary? Hump. I'm at Jim Hardman's place."

I closed the bedroom door and looked at the sofa. He'd folded the linens and the blanket and placed the pillow on top of the stack. I started to take them into the bedroom and changed my mind. No way I wanted to listen to what they had to say. I went into the kitchen and made myself another coffee to replace the cup I'd left in the bedroom.

"Rosemary's coming over," he said. He stopped in the doorway and looked at me.

"You want the bedroom or the living room for the conference?"

"Dumb," Hump said, "real dumb."

That was a fair estimate. I said, "I don't know where my head is this year." The phone rang in the bedroom and I edged past him and got a tap on the shoulder from him.

"Your line's been busy," Art said.

"Hump's been using it." I was about to add that he'd been using it for his courting but that wouldn't roll off my tongue. Anyway, he'd remained in the kitchen so it would have been a broken needle.

"You got the green bottle yet?"

"The Ansley Mall store doesn't open until ten."

"I'll have to trust you," Art said. "The Carl Culp you asked about. He's an open case."

"What?"

"He turned up dead last month. The fourteenth of last month."

"How?"

"Somebody broke his neck. And he'd been beaten with something. Not a whip or a rope. Something harder."

"Chains? The way bikers use them?"

"Might be," Art said.

"Where?"

"Let me see." I could hear paper crackle. "You know the underground parking lot at the Omni? Found in his car the morning after one of those big rock concerts, one of the English groups."

"How'd your people figure it?"

"The big guess was that it was a drug ripoff. They found about half a pound of low-grade grass under the front seat. You know how that got put together."

I knew. If you didn't have anything else to go on and there was dope involved, they always figured it was some disagreement over the dope or the money. It was standard.

"You haven't told me your interest in this," Art said.

"That information you gave Hump last night."

"The biker gang?"

"Yeah. The Atlanta Outlanders. Hump asked them a question and got a strange answer. He wanted to find Culp and got told to light a candle for him."

Art was a practicing Catholic. He understood the candle bit. "It might be worth some more questions."

"I understand there was some trouble at the Majestic last night. Might be those Outlanders are in your slammer right now."

"Who gets asked the questions?"

I called Hump to the phone. "Give him descriptions of Shorty and Curly."

After Hump finished, he passed the phone back to me. Art said, "I think you just ruined my breakfast."

"Think how pleased the Captain'll be when you crack the case."

"Crack the case? Oh, shit."

"Isn't that the way real cops talk?"

"Oh, hell, yes."

"Four this afternoon at my place?"

"You'll have the green bottle?"

"With the seal still on it," I said.

After I shaved and showered, I sat at the kitchen table and started a grocery list. I got past eggs, bacon, bread and milk, and I was considering some Italian sausages and a few steaks when I heard the car door slam out in the drive.

Hump opened the door and let Rosemary in. She was wearing dark slacks, a white turtleneck and the suede coat from the day before. I left my grocery list and went in to have my look at her. Hump closed the door and stood with his back to it.

"That a rental car out there?"

Rosemary said that it was.

"Lend it to me for an hour," Hump said.

While she fumbled for the keys, Hump worked his shoulders into his topcoat. "I forgot to tell you, Jim. I made a second call. Got myself an appointment with a doctor at the Medical Arts Building. I thought I'd better have this neck looked at."

"Your neck?" Rosemary whirled from Hump to me. I could see the concern in her face. "What happened …?"

"I think it was some folk medicine Jim tried on me." Hump took the keys and left.

Rosemary unbuttoned her coat. Maybe it was reflex. I went over and helped her with it. That was that southern gentleman crap, hard to shake after you've done it for years. Close up, I could smell her perfume. It was something subtle, there and almost not there, and it rocked me. I quickstepped away from her. I'd headed for the bedroom with the coat before I had a second thought. I was going to drop the coat on the foot of the bed. *No way.* Her perfume was in the coat. It stayed on my bed long enough and I'd be sleeping the next day or two with the scent of her.

"What happened to Hump's neck?"

I dropped the suede coat at the end of the sofa. "That's his story. Wouldn't want to spoil it for him."

"You two seem to like secrets."

I shrugged. "I'm coffee'd out, but if you want some …"

"Thank you," she said. "I would."

She followed me into the kitchen and watched while I filled the kettle and placed it over the flame. "I'm glad you're going to help."

"Did Hump say that?"

"Not in so many words," she admitted.

I let that float in the air for a few seconds. In the end I said, "I guess I am. Among other things, I had a dream about you last night."

"I hope it was a good dream."

I could see her eyes, nothing but her eyes. The warm amusement there. "It was tiring."

Then she was laughing. It was warm and real and throaty. And I knew that she thought I meant the dream had been a sexual one. It hadn't been and I was about to say, no, it wasn't a wet dream, lady. I saw the absurdity of that and I backed away.

After all, some dreams are private.

The hook was in and I might as well try to swallow it. You fought it and it tore some guts out. I grinned at her and made her that cup of coffee.

CHAPTER SIX

"One mistake you made there," I said. "If you'd told the police the truth the first time, there's a good chance they'd have found Carl Culp and your daughter."

"I've made more than one mistake." She'd settled into my easy chair. I was off to one side, watching her in profile most of the time. I'd always thought that women in their thirties who wore turtlenecks had something to hide. Not Rosemary. Her throat had a good clean line.

"Hump told me."

"That Billie Joe was illegitimate?"

I nodded.

"I was seventeen. Buddy was twenty-two. He was an assistant buyer for one of the big tobacco companies. He said he loved me, he said a lot of interesting things, but he didn't say he was already married."

It was the traveling salesman and the farmer's daughter story. This time without the funny punchline.

"Billie Joe was four when Charles was transferred from New York to manage the zipper factory. By then I'd been to business college and I was working in the shipping department office. He'd been divorced two or three years before and he didn't trust women very much. It took him almost three months to work up the nerve to ask me out and it was another three or four months before he told me he loved me. I'm not sure whether I loved him or not. Still, he treated me well and he was good to Billie Joe."

"Until you told him the truth about Billie Joe."

"How did you know?"

"It's between the lines," I said.

"Charles believed I was divorced. That was what I'd told them when I applied for the job at the zipper factory. After he got interested in me, it was easy enough for him to look at the personnel records."

"You told him and he blew?"

"It was a nightmare," Rosemary said. "I'd never been through anything like it. He called me a whore, a rotten, stinking whore. It didn't matter to him that I'd been seventeen at the time. Nothing mattered."

I felt the dryness slip in. "But he loved you enough to forgive you."

"He forgave me."

I did the math in my head. That had been thirteen or fourteen years ago and I could imagine that life. He gave her everything she wanted. All the material things. And perhaps in his own way he loved her. The trouble was that he couldn't trust her. He watched her and waited for the mistake to be repeated. He waited for the seventeen-year-old girl to reappear. And when that didn't happen he turned from her to the little girl. He looked for the seams and veins, the faults and cracks, for the evidence that the mother would be reborn in the child.

"About a year ago there was an especially violent scene between Charles and Billie Joe. She was an hour late coming back from a Christmas dance. The violence of it stunned her. As soon as I could get her away from him, I had to do something. I tried to explain it to her. I told her about me and about her father. Oh, of course, she knew that Charles wasn't her father but she didn't know about Buddy."

She lifted her purse and placed it on her knees. She didn't have to dig far. She brought out an envelope and passed it to me. I gave the outside of the envelope a look. The return address was that of Carl Culp with the Argonne address. The postmark, like most of them, was blurred, but I could read enough of it to see that the letter had been mailed in July. I opened the envelope and found a folded strip of newsprint. It had been clipped from the first part of the want ads. Down near the bottom of the strip, under Personal Interests, one item had been circled with a red ink.

Wanted: any information about the whereabouts of Wallace (Buddy) James.

Below that there was a box number at the *Constitution*.

"I found that in her dresser after I gave up looking for Billie Joe here in Atlanta and returned to Kingstree."

"No letter with it?"

"If there was," Rosemary said, "she either destroyed it or brought it to Atlanta with her."

I folded the newsprint and shoved it back in the envelope. I returned it to her on the way past. I went into the kitchen and scattered eggshells and toast crumbs all over the floor, digging the morning paper out of the trash. I found the want ads section and checked the Personal Interests part of it. The ad wasn't there. I hadn't expected it to be. July to December was a long time to pay the rates. And my guess was that they'd received an answer or given up. I balled up the paper and stuffed it back in the can.

"Any special reason for them to look for him here in Atlanta?" I returned to the living room.

"The best," she said. "The last time I heard from Buddy he was living here."

"When was that?" I got my smokes from the coffee table and lit one.

"The year I moved to Kingstree and went to work at the zipper factory. Somehow, I don't know how, he found out where I was. After that, it wasn't hard. I'd taken James as a last name."

"Fifteen or sixteen years ago?"

"About that."

"And when you met him, when you were seventeen?"

"He lived in Durham."

"All right. He found you. When you saw him did he tell you what he was doing for a living?"

"I didn't see him. And I didn't talk to him long. He called long distance. I told him that I wasn't interested in seeing him."

I got the phone book from the bedroom, the white pages, and carried it into the living room. I flipped through it until I found the JAMES listings. There were about two solid pages of them. There wasn't a Wallace James. Down near the bottom there was a W this and a W that. I creased the section with a fingernail and passed the book to her. "Any of those that might be the right one?"

"His middle initial was A for Arnold." She returned the book to me.

I saw what she meant. There was no W. A. James in the book.

Impasse. The roadblock was up.

Hump returned a few minutes later. I'd expected him to be wearing a neck brace. He wasn't. He looked about the same, though he did seem to have a bit more movement.

"What'd the doc say?"

"From now on, when I need a rubdown, I'd be better off going to one of those places on Houston Street."

"A comic," I said.

"And a pickpocket."

"Hit you good, huh?"

"With X-rays and all? There went the booze money for the week."

"That reminds me." I looked at Rosemary who'd picked up her suede coat.

"You coming in?"

"It looks that way."

Hump leaned toward me and lowered his voice. "I've already set the money deal with her."

"Good enough." I passed him and helped her with her coat. The collar caught a few strands of her hair and I wanted to reach out and touch it and pull it free. I didn't. I turned away. Her soft, "Thank you, James," caught at me and I got the coffee cup and carried it into the kitchen. I came back and watched her and Hump. She'd started out the door when Hump laughed and handed her the car keys.

"Might as well drive," he said.

She thanked him but her eyes weren't on him. They burned the thirty feet or so from the front door to the kitchen doorway. I felt an itch on my forehead. Another few seconds and I knew I'd break out in a sweat.

"Good-bye, James."

Hump closed the door behind her.

"The neck all right?"

"Bruised, no breaks or cracks."

"You up for a bit of work?"

"After lunch?"

"Maybe," I said. "You flunked a good part of the test…"

"You never did grade me."

"… so let's see how you handled the money matters."

"For the two of us a thousand a week. Five hundred each."

"You get an advance?"

"The first week."

"Then I think we ought to have lunch downtown, somewhere near the main library." I got my topcoat from the bedroom closet. When I returned to the living room, he had his money roll in his hand. He fanned out five hundred for me. I took it and shoved it in my pocket.

"Remember the doctor visit. That goes down on expenses."

"It's written down."

We drove to the Plaza so he could pick up his Buick. Then I followed him to his apartment house. He left the Buick in the parking lot and we drove downtown and parked in the Davison's parking deck.

On the elevator headed down to the street level, I said, "Only four shopping days to Christmas."

"You just notice that?"

"In the morning paper."

"What you giving Marcy?"

"Unless I do some shopping in the next four days, only my poor tired body," I said.

He grinned. "That's what every girl secretly wants for Christmas."

"Remember you said that. Remember the date. December twentieth."

We stepped out the elevator and pushed our way through a crowd of shoppers in the small lobby. It was windy and cold on the street and we were a block or two away from the main branch of the library. Research first, I decided. Lunch after that.

I knew where the City Directories were. Thirteen or fourteen years ago: that was the last time Rosemary had heard from Buddy James. I started with the 1961 book. I found the listing.

"Wallace, A. (Emily P.) commod, broker. 211 Meadow Way Drive."

I showed the listing to Hump. I took the 1962 and he took the 1963. Wallace James was in both. The same with 1964 and 1965; 1966 and 1967, still there.

We didn't find him in 1968. I went through 1975 before I gave it up.

That was it. Somewhere between 1967 and 1968 Buddy James had left town. And he hadn't returned.

We split on the corner of Forsyth, outside the library. Hump headed up Forsyth toward Fairlie. Emile's French Restaurant was on Fairlie. I walked down Peachtree the block or so to Davison's Department Store.

It was crowded. The main floor is devoted to women's stuff, perfume and make-up and bags. Other things like that. I wandered about in the shopping hysteria for ten minutes or so. The new five hundred in my pocket and I thought I might buy the first of the five or six presents I'd get for Marcy.

It didn't happen that way. All around me people were trying to get waited on. Every time I stopped to look at some perfume or a leather handbag, two or three clerks would rush to me and offer to help me. The third time this happened, I realized that they'd tabbed me as a possible shoplifter.

That bothered me. I left Davison's and joined Hump at Emile's. He was on his second drink and holding a table for us. I ordered a cognac to shake the cold wind and looked at the menu.

"Buy anything?"

"It was all I could do to get out of there without being arrested."

"It's that season," Hump said.

"Saw two blacks in an argument with a salesgirl. One of the blacks had a fancy silk scarf wrapped around his neck. He was telling the girl all he was doing was taking the scarf back to the men's section so that he could see himself in the big mirror."

"And the other one saying that that was right, man?"

I nodded.

We both ordered the lemon sole.

Meadow Way Drive was one of those little streets that run off Twenty-sixth and Peachtree Road. Back there, off the main way, it is a mixture of small, exclusive apartment houses and homes that look like they might run in the high money. Lawns seem to take up most of the plot, the houses built almost against the back property line.

I parked in front of 211 and turned to Hump. He was staring past me at the house. It was brick, that English-manor style. The front yard wasn't exactly a lawn. It was a patch of ivy that ran from the sidewalk to the front steps. The way I felt about ivy it could have been kudzu for all I cared.

"I'll wait out here," Hump said.

"Some reason?"

"Lots of snakes in ivy," he said.

I knew that wasn't true. He'd had his look at the neighborhood and decided it was too all white. What one mayor had called "the city too busy to hate" still had some time on its hands in certain sections of town. If Hump knocked on the door in this part of town, he'd better be carrying a clipboard and saying he wanted to read the gas meter.

"Whatever." I walked up the stone path to the porch. I fumbled about, looking for a doorbell. Finally I decided the brass door knocker wasn't just ornamental. I gave it a bang or two and stepped back. The door opened a couple of minutes later. A dumpy little black woman peered out at me. She wasn't wearing a maid's uniform, but there was an apron tied around her waist and she was wearing a hair net. Passing her, blowing on the warm air that rushed out to the cold, there was the smell of turnips or some other kind of greens.

"Yes, sir?"

"I'd like to see the lady of the house." I reached into my coat pocket and brought out one of my new business cards. It was the same old scam. The card represented me as an agent for Nationwide Insurance. It was the new batch of cards. I'd used my last of the old ones back in the fall. This time I'd spent more cash and had raised black letters added. It was supposed to be twice as impressive.

"She won't want to buy any," the black lady said.

"I'm not selling insurance," I said. "I'm trying to trace someone who owned this home some years back. A Mister Wallace James."

"What is it, Netta?"

The black lady said, "Excuse me," and closed the door on me. I waited. It was a shaded porch and the temperature seemed about ten degrees lower than it had been out on the walk. I turned and looked the length of the street. A frail old man was walking two poodles near the junction of Twenty-sixth. The poodles were trying to decide if it was too cold for their outdoor business or not.

The door opened wider this time. "Miz Butler'll see you for a minute."

I followed the black lady through a dark hallway and into a large living room. The smell of cooking was stronger now. Off to the left of the living room, I could see the dining room. There was one place set and lunch was just over. I decided that I'd interrupted Netta when she'd been clearing the table.

A thin lady in her seventies sat in a straight-backed chair near the living room fireplace. A gas log burned on high. It wasn't needed. The thermostat must have been sitting on eighty degrees.

Her skin was pale, like new parchment. Her hair, that bluish tint, was loose and girlish. When I was a few feet away from her, she lifted my business card and strained to read it. "Please have a chair, Mr. Hardman."

I unbuttoned my topcoat but didn't take it off. I sat in the chair she'd indicated with a nod of her head. I saw that, though she might be in her seventies, it hadn't crooked her back yet. She sat very straight, in the proper posture, her small feet together, her knees touching.

"Netta said you weren't selling insurance."

"Not this time," I said, "but I could send someone over next week if you're interested in coverage."

"I believe my affairs are in order," she said. Behind that tone there was a hint of lawyers and banks and trusts.

"I'll make this as brief as I can," I said. "A Mrs. Ethel Turner, a widow with no dependents and no close family there, died recently in Durham, North Carolina. She has a brother but they have not been in touch with each other for a number of years. I think there must have been some kind of family dispute."

"That is sad, Mr. Hardman."

"Sometimes this is a sad business," I said, matching her tone. "A bit over a year ago, Mrs. Turner had second thoughts about her brother. That came about with the death of her husband. The local office contacted her and she was informed that she had no living beneficiary. Her decision was that her brother was to be that beneficiary. I suppose she intended to reconcile herself with her brother. Of course, she was ill during this time and she didn't realize she would pass away so soon. People never do." It was all I could do not to smile. I knew I sounded like someone out of a Jane Austen novel. "People always believe they have more time left than they do."

Her smile was sly, earthy. "Are you certain you're not selling insurance today?"

"Boy Scout honor," I said. "Our problem is that the last address, the one she gave on the form 2323, the change of beneficiary, had her brother living here." I waved a hand at her living room.

"I don't know if I can help you. My late husband bought this home in 1967. I don't even think I met the former owner ..."

"Mr. Wallace James," I said.

"... except that one time at the closing."

"There might be some way to trace him through the sale," I said. "Did your husband pay cash for the home?"

"I believe we assumed the mortgage. And, of course, when my husband passed away, the remainder of the mortgage was paid off by the insurance."

"Do you remember the mortgage company?"

"It was Green Brothers," she said. "It is one of the largest in the city."

I nodded and stood up. I was sweating from the heat in the room. It was time to get out where I could take a deep breath without steaming my lungs. "I appreciate you seeing me, Mrs. Butler."

"Was it a very large amount?" she asked, about the time I reached the hallway arch.

"The insurance policy? It was twenty-five thousand."

"That won't go far in these times," she said.

"Every bit helps," I said.

The black lady, Netta, sprinted from the dining room and reached the front door ahead of me. She was opening the door when I heard Mrs. Butler call me. "Mr. Hardman?"

I returned to the living room doorway. "Yes, ma'am?"

"After the closing I remember my husband saying that … what was his name?"

"Mr. James."

"That Mr. James planned to move to the country and take up some kind of farming. I remember because my husband said that if Mr. James couldn't get ahead in the city, he certainly wouldn't in the country."

"Thank you, ma'am." Netta waited for me at the door. She swung it open. I gave her a suggestion of a bow and a right-eyed wink on the way past.

I crossed the parking lot of the Peachtree Hills Liquor Store and placed the bagged bottle in the seat between Hump and me. It was the green bottle of Courvoisier and it had, at the cash register, done bad damage to a twenty and a ten.

"Write in the expense book," I said. "Cognac for Art Maloney at $28.79."

"After that … do I put down *bribe?*"

"A curious idea," I said.

We had an hour to waste. Hump slumped in the easy chair and sucked at a beer bottle. I looked up Green Brothers in the white pages and copied the address on Marietta Street. Below that, I wrote down the address on Meadow Way and the Butler name.

I had the green bottle on the coffee table when Art arrived. I'd left the price tag on. He dropped his coat on the sofa and grinned at me with that big round Irish face of it. He picked up the bottle and, with a thumbnail, peeled away the price tag and dropped it in the ashtray. "Leaving price tags on, that's not very polite."

"Missed that," I said. "Crack any big cases today?"

"Funny you should ask that." He turned away and placed the bottle on top of his coat. "The answer is no."

"No?"

"Not when I left this morning. But it was rocking around the edges. Shorty and Curly were howling for their lawyers."

"You talk to them?"

He nodded. "Until the day shift came on. A lot of *I don't knows* and *I don't remembers* bouncing off those walls."

"You get a feeling?"

"Nothing I can make a charge on," Art said. "But they know more about Culp than they're telling."

"If you talk to them this evening...?"

"Yeah?"

"See if they know anything about a young blond girl named Billie Joe, who might have been with Culp a time or two."

"Another favor, huh?"

Hump grinned. "You ought to see the lady talked him into it."

"Since when did Jim need talking into something that had money in it?"

"Changed my morals," I said. "I'm twice-born, twice-born."

"And ready to testify now?"

We laughed. I'd told him about that years ago and he still remembered. That was the religious con they pulled on soldiers and sailors out in California. It was during the Korean one and I'd been in transit. It would happen a day or two before the payday. Nobody'd have a dime. The notice would go up on the board. WANTED TWENTY SERVICEMEN TO GO TO A PARTY. You'd get there and it would be cookies and punch in the rec room of some church. There'd be some pretty girls who'd play Ping-pong with you and then you'd notice everybody drifting toward the chapel and you'd get herded that way too. And, suddenly, those pretty girls would get up and testify about what the Lord had done for them. Then they'd sit down, pleased with themselves, and stare at you. Now it's your turn, they'd seem to be saying.

"Billie Joe?" Art got out his notepad and wrote the name down.

"That's right."

He closed the book. "If I can fit it into the conversation." He stood and picked up the green bottle and his coat. "I'll leave now if there's nothing else you want me to do for you."

"Now that you ask." I passed him the paper with the Green Brothers and Wallace James and the address on Meadow Way on it. "On your way home, you might stop by the Green Brothers and find out if they've got an address on this James dude. Might be, after he sold the house to the Butlers, he moved to the country and took up farming."

Art stared at the Green Brothers address. "Marietta Street is not on my way home."

"Might be you can crack another case," I said.

"Oh, shit." Art lifted the bottle and looked at it. "If I had any sense, I'd pour this down your drain and forget the whole thing."

"Don't do that. That stuff is sixteen or seventeen years old. My drain's not used to that kind of quality."

"Which case is this?"

"The woman killed at the 7-11 Wednesday night."

"Ellison's working on that one," Art said.

"He doesn't love me like you do."

"And you can't follow this out yourself?"

I shook my head. I didn't have to say it. He knew my scams. That insurance agent thing would work with some old lady. Green Brothers might call the local office and check on me.

Art struggled into his topcoat. "I'll see."

"That means a maybe?"

"That means I'll head in the direction of downtown and see if I get there. That's no promise."

It was as much as I could hope for. I let it go.

After Art left, Hump said, "You're getting your money's worth on that bottle."

That was true enough. But it was a damned good bottle of cognac.

The wait was a red hair short of an hour. I made it to the phone on the second ring.

"This pays off the whole bottle of brandy?"

I said that it did.

"At the closing, Wallace James gave Green Brothers an address in Plainsville. Broad Street 455. That what you want?"

"Kiss, kiss and thank you, Art."

"Tomorrow's a Sunday, a day of rest. Don't call me."

"What if the bikers know something about Billie Joe?"

"I'll call you."

He hung up. I got the white pages and dialed the Riviera and asked for Rosemary's room. When she came on the line, I offered her a Sunday drive into the country.

She accepted.

CHAPTER SEVEN

It was a cold, bright Sunday morning.

I'd said I'd pick up Rosemary at ten and I was there on time. I might have been early if I'd forgotten a promise I'd made the night before. That I'd rake out the old Ford. It took about ten minutes. Beer cans and bottles, those plastic glasses some of the bars use, cigarette packs, parts of newspapers, Braves, Hawks and Falcon programs, some green chicken bones...and a lot more. The *lot more* was dirt and dust mainly.

Rosemary waited for me in the Riviera lobby. She was wearing a green and brown tweed pants suit. When I approached her with the idea of helping her with her coat, she smiled and shook her head. She unfolded a black serape with some kind of Indian design on it and slipped her head through the yoke.

Her smile had some imp in it. "Do I look like a hippie, James?"

"Call me Jim." I took her elbow and turned her toward the main entrance. "If you look like a hippie, you'll give them a good name."

We were a few miles from the motel, heading toward Buckhead, when the Coors can rolled from under the front seat and stopped at the toe of her right boot. She leaned over and picked it up.

I remembered. That went back to the previous spring. A newspaperman I knew and his wife had driven to Oklahoma to visit her family and they'd brought me back a case.

"Somebody must have tossed it through my window," I said.

She placed it on the seat next to her bag. "Of course, Jim."

It was an hour's drive through the winter landscape. I liked it. I felt myself bubbling away. It wasn't just that Rosemary was with me. It's the way my head is put on backward. I like the gray, the bareness, the dormant things. All the promises that spring is making from underground. And, I think, I'm disappointed when the green rush comes.

Plainsville is on the edge of the soybean country. The market for soybeans in the last few years has meant a lot to the farmers. It's close to a constant in the changing farm market. I suspect all the farmers in the area begin grace by saying, "Thank the Lord for soy sauce and bean curd."

The town doesn't show any sign of the new money. The two-block main street is chipping, flaking and rotting from the outside. What's there is a parody of the southern small town. There are a couple of seed and feed stores, a hardware store, a Woolworth's, a supermarket and a movie theater. The movie house is showing one of those made-in-Georgia films. The low-budget ones with lots of car racing and moonshine making and nubile girls wearing costumes that look like they were pirated out of a comic script. The film listed at the Lyric, as we drive by, is *White Whiskey Run,* starring nobody at all.

And there's an old hotel that might have been fancy back in the 1930s. Half of it has been painted an off white and the other half has been scraped and wire brushed. There's an A-frame sign on the lawn in front. NOW SERVING LUNCH.

I waved at the sign. "Lunch later?"

Rosemary leaned past me to look at the hotel. "Fried chicken, baking powder biscuits and greens?"

"And country ham, sweet potatoes, string beans and apple pie and ice cream for dessert."

"You make it sound good." She leaned away, settling into her seat once more.

"And don't forget cornbread and spoonbread and buttermilk and iced tea."

"I accept the invitation," she said.

"Lunch is on me, the Rolaids are on you."

After the two-block main street, the car dealerships and the heavy-machinery franchises flanked both sides of the road.

The house was squat, one floored, built out of cinderblock and trimmed with red brick. Except for the picture window off to the right and the brick trim, it might have been a World War Two pillbox. There were pyracantha bushes crowding the house, below the picture window and along the small porch. The red berries gave the yard the only color it had.

I parked out front and gave the numbers on the mailbox next to the street a check. It matched. It was the right one. I waited, giving Rosemary some time. After a minute or so, when she didn't move, I said, "You nervous?"

"I guess I am."

"You can wait in the car if you want to."

"No, I'm not nervous for the reason you think. That's done. It was over years ago."

I nodded and got out and walked around and opened the door for her. The wind was strong and there was the scent of ice in it. She took her time. She removed the serape and folded it and placed it on the car seat before I closed the door. As we went up the walk, I watched her smooth her hair.

I reached the porch before the thought occurred to me. It was church time. There was always the chance that Wallace James was already in his pew, settling in for his morning nap.

I pressed the doorbell anyway.

A man opened the door and peered out at us. I put his age a few years past forty. He wore a gray sweater over a blue flannel shirt. He was thin and stoop-shouldered. His hair was cut skin tight, what we used to call an onion-peeling, and it was mainly gray with a sprinkling of the original black.

"Yes?"

I turned slightly and looked at Rosemary. I wanted to see how she reacted. Her face didn't show anything and there was no recognition on the man's face. "I'd like to see Wallace James if he's here."

"He don't live here."

"This is the address I was given," I said.

"Is it business?"

"Not exactly," I said. "We're from Atlanta."

"He don't have office hours on Sunday," the man said. "Weekdays you can see him at the Forrest Building on Main Street."

His eyes had shifted from me. He was looking at Rosemary.

Rosemary stepped closer to the door. "I'm Rosemary Atkinson. I knew Wallace ... Buddy ... a long time ago."

"You're that woman, the one from South Carolina?"

"Yes, I am." It was hard for the words to come out. There was a harshness in his voice that must have disturbed her. *That* woman.

"Then I guess you're here about the girl, about Billie Joe."

"Yes."

I put a hand on the doorframe and leaned between them. "Billie Joe in town now?"

"You Mr. Atkinson?"

"No." I'd started to lie but changed my mind. There wasn't any way to know whether saying I was Charles Atkinson would be a plus or a minus.

"I need to talk to Buddy," Rosemary said.

"I guess you do." He looked over his shoulder and then back at us. "I can't see the clock from here. You got the time?"

I checked my watch. "It's 11:25," I said.

"He's at the cemetery," the man said.

The question must have been written on my forehead.

"It's Grave Sunday," he said.

"Where's the cemetery?"

He stepped onto the porch. He pointed to the left, back toward town, the direction from which we'd come. "See that white spire?"

I said I did.

"That's the Methodist church. The town graveyard's behind it."

"Thank you." I watched him move back inside the house. "I didn't get your name."

"Bob James," he said. "I'm Buddy's brother."

"Mr. James, was Billie Joe here?"

"That's not my business. You talk to Buddy."

He didn't close the door. He waited. I took Rosemary's arm and we walked to the car. After I closed the car door on the passenger side, I looked at the house. I had a flash of a gray stone face, his face, and then he closed the door.

"Odd time for it," I said.

Rosemary slipped the serape over her head. "What?"

"Grave cleaning," I said. "I thought that was usually in the spring."

"I don't think I know …"

"It's a back country relic," I said. "Must go back a hundred years or so. Most places it's half picnic and half work. The church sets aside one Sunday a year and they clean up all the graves, their own and those of ones who don't have family left."

Beginning two blocks from the church all the spaces were taken. A good part of them were filled by pickup trucks. I had to go three blocks past the church before I found an opening large enough for my Ford. On the way around the front of the car I blew out a breath and watched it condense. It wasn't a good day for a picnic.

From blocks away I could hear the chomp-chomp of the hoes and rakes. It was probably hard digging in that cold ground. The sound reminded me of something else: cool mornings, chopping cotton before the hot sun came out.

A path by the side of the church led to the cemetery. There were lights on in the basement of the church and I stopped and looked in. The small children were at Sunday school. That explained why there wasn't any shouting, any noise of game-playing.

Past the back of the church, the graveyard spread out before us. It was level in front and rising, rolling, toward the back. A hundred or so men and women and teen-agers, in work clothes, labored over the graves. Hoes and rakes ripped the grass and weeds away. Wheelbarrows moved down the paths between the headstones. The piles of grass and weeds were scooped up on shovels and tamped into the barrows. It was work done in almost silence, grunting, low voices and the noise of the tools.

One man stood out at the edge of the swirl of movement. He was tall and white-haired and his jeans and denim shirt seemed store-bought new. That and the fact that he wore a black tie tagged him as the preacher.

"You see him?"

Rosemary shook her head. I took her arm and led her toward the tall man in the new work clothes. When we were a couple of steps away he turned toward us and smiled. I was right. He was the preacher. I knew that kindly smile. I think they taught it at Preacher College.

"Brother." He held out his hand and I took it. "Sister." He leaned past me and offered his hand to Rosemary. That over, he allowed himself a teasing remark. "I see you didn't come dressed to work."

"The truth is we're from out of town. We're looking for Buddy James."

"Buddy?" He spun about slowly. "I know he's here. I don't see him now. I suppose he's at the James plot." He lifted his hand and pointed toward the high ground at the right rear of the cemetery. "Over there."

I thanked him and took Rosemary's elbow. As we moved away he invited us to stay for church. I said we might and then we passed through the oldest part of the graveyard. The head-stones there were so weathered that I could hardly read them. I guessed that was because most of these early stones were cut from limestone.

Along the way people stopped working and stared at us. I think we were a curiosity of sorts. City people, I could almost hear them say. And then we were on the high ground and I felt the stiffness in Rosemary. I let my hand drop away.

"I see him," she said.

"Where?"

"There."

A man on his knees with his back to us. He was using one of those claw-like hand tools. The grave he was clearing appeared newer than the others nearby. It was still rounded, not sunken yet. He worked without wasted movement. Grass dug out and swept to the side, earth patted back in place.

He was wearing what might have been, at one time, the pants to a dark brown suit. The seat was shiny down to the knees and there were smears of white paint on the sides near the pockets. He wore an elbows-out blue sweater and a tan canvas rainhat. Shaggy brown hair damp-curled from under the hat.

Rosemary walked away from me. I waited. He didn't notice her until he saw her shadow. He looked up and said, "Are you ...?" and got to his feet. I had a look at his face. It was flushed, sweat pocked. I knew he had high blood pressure then and I had a feeling he'd almost fainted when he saw her.

"Yes, Buddy."

"I think I was half expecting you." He looked at me. "Is this your husband?"

"No."

I stepped closer and watched him brush the dirt from his right hand. "I'm Jim Hardman."

"Mr. Hardman is an ex-policeman," Rosemary said. "He's helping me look for Billie Joe."

"Look for her?" His face darkened even more with a new rush of blood. "Isn't she with you?"

"No, Buddy."

"But I thought she'd ..." He broke off. "I guess we'd better talk."

They walked downhill toward the church. I remained behind long enough to read the headstone.

Emily Parker James
Beloved Wife of Wallace
1929–1970

I filled a styrofoam cup at the pot in the church kitchen and joined them at a table in the dining room. It was filled with long trestle tables and I guess this was where they had those church suppers. I'd expected to find a sugar bowl on the table. There wasn't one. I sipped the coffee straight.

"You were hard to find, Buddy."

"That was what Billie Joe said. Almost exactly."

The coffee was harsh and mean. "When was that, Mr. James?"

"The night she left Rosemary at the hotel."

"Carl Culp was with her?"

"Sure," he said. "He set up the meeting."

"Then you saw the ad in the newspaper?"

"Not exactly," he said. "A friend who still lives in Atlanta saw the item in the personals and sent it to me."

He was talking to me but looking at Rosemary. There was a jerky, foolish grin on his face. "And you contacted Carl Culp?"

"No, I had Fred ... Fred Thompson ... he's a lawyer ... answer the ad. Fred passed the word back to me that my daughter, Billie Joe, wanted to see me. Of course, I wanted to see her too and we arranged the meeting that night." He shook his head slowly. "I think I believed you'd be with her, Rosemary."

"I would have if she'd asked me," Rosemary said.

"After I talked to her, I realized why she hadn't asked you. You see, she wanted to meet me so that she could decide whether she wanted to come and live with me."

"I don't believe that, Buddy."

"Believe it or not, it's true. She said she felt like she was in prison and she wanted out of it. She had nothing but angry things to say about your husband, Charles."

"And about me?"

"She wasn't that harsh about you. She said she thought you'd sold yourself for security and it hadn't made you happy."

It was edging toward soap opera. Another few minutes and they'd be crying together and comforting each other. I changed the direction of it. "The night you met her she was with Carl Culp?"

He nodded. "Fred Thompson was with me. Fred said there were some legal aspects to this and I'd better protect myself. I didn't agree with him but I was glad for his company. I was, I guess, afraid to meet her for the first time."

"And at that meeting ...?"

"We talked. She said she wanted to go home with me. Fred didn't think that was wise. He and Billie Joe had a heck of an argument about it. I remember Billie Joe said she was eighteen and she was grown and she could live anywhere she wanted to."

Another sip of the coffee. "And that convinced Fred?"

"Not really, but he agreed it might be okay if I called Rosemary and told her that Billie Joe was with me."

"But you didn't call," Rosemary said.

"She wouldn't let me. She talked me out of it. As soon as we got to the farm I wanted to call you. She said if I made that call, she'd leave and I'd never hear from her again. So I put it off. I thought she'd change her mind. She didn't. In fact, she only stayed three or four days because of me wanting to call Rosemary. She caught me one morning while I was trying to place a call to Atlanta. She got angry and screamed at me. That was Tuesday or Wednesday. I thought she'd calmed down. When I left for my office, I took her with me. She needed some clothing. I gave her some money and she was supposed to stop by my office after she finished shopping. When she didn't, I went looking for her. On a hunch I stopped by Bud's Service Station. That's where the bus stops. Bud said a girl answering Billie Joe's description had bought a ticket for Atlanta and she'd got on the 4:55 bus."

"That was the last you heard from her?"

"From her, yes. But not about her. Later that night Fred called me from Atlanta. He said Billie Joe hadn't been able to reach Carl Culp and, since she didn't know anybody else in town, she'd called him. Fred said he would help her if he could and he would try to talk her into getting in touch with Rosemary."

"And...?"

"He thought he'd talked her into it. He said he bought her a bus ticket to Kingstree and he gave her some spending money and dropped her off at the bus station downtown." He'd finished his coffee. Now he was breaking the cup into bits and shreds. "That's why I'm surprised to see you, Rosemary. I thought she was with you."

"She isn't."

It was done. There wasn't that much more to say. "I'll need Fred Thompson's address and phone number. I might need to talk to him."

"I'm sure he'll be glad to tell you all he knows."

He wrote the address and phone number in my notebook. I put that away and collected the three cups. I found a trash basket and dropped them in it. When I started back for the table, they were leaning together, talking. I stopped a few feet away. "I'll wait for you in front of the church, Rosemary."

I walked to the Ford and got it turned about and drove to the church entrance. She came out five or six minutes later and got in before I could open the car door for her.

There wasn't much to talk about. Both of us knew the words and neither of us had to say them. It wasn't as simple as she'd thought it was. It was complex and strange.

Yes, I said in my mind, that girl came close to hating your guts. She wanted to hurt you all she could.

And she was saying that that wasn't true. Billie Joe loved her and she'd liked Charles most of the time.

Back and forth. Back and forth.

A few miles out of Atlanta a cold icy rain began to fall.

CHAPTER EIGHT

I t was a few minutes before two in the afternoon when I pulled into the driveway that led past the main entrance to the Riviera. There were two private cars and a Yellow Cab in the line in front of us. The light icy rain was still falling and it was messy out on the roads.

The silent talking between us, that she'd put back her head and closed her eyes, made the drive back from Plainsville seem longer than it really was.

One of the cars moved away. The line moved up one car length. "I suppose you have other things to do this afternoon," she said finally.

"Not really."

"Nothing?" Her face was pale and chilled. She looked drained.

"A call to Fred Thompson. If there's a football game on the tube, I'll watch some of that and have a drink or three. And I'll have supper."

"Alone?"

"What?"

"Supper alone?"

I said, "Yes."

"Hump told me about your girl."

"Marcy," I said. "She's out of town until some time Wednesday night."

The other car pulled away from the entrance. The Yellow Cab moved up. We were close enough so that Rosemary could turn and look into the lobby. "I don't think I can stand another day in that room."

"Don't then."

"Is that an invitation?"

I pulled away from the curb and passed the Yellow Cab. I grinned at her and watched some color return to her face. "It's either an invitation or this is a kidnapping."

I pushed the grocery cart to the bread section of the Superior Food Store on North Highland. She walked beside me and watched while I tossed in a couple of loaves of sourdough french bread. "That's the first clue."

"Is it something special?"

"Ethnic," I said. "I am an ethnic chef."

At the dairy shelf I threw in a pound of butter. "That's number two."

"It could be anything at all."

I returned with a large can of peeled tomatoes.

"Spaghetti?"

"Everybody makes that. It's too easy."

A package of garlic. A small jar of feta cheese. A tin of olive oil. A pound and a half of frozen peeled and deveined shrimp. "That's it."

"All of it?"

"Except for a bottle of white wine I've already got."

On the way across the parking lot I said, "Give up?"

"Yes, Jim."

"You're no fun."

The drive toward home. I guess I'd been expecting it sooner or later. "You didn't ask what Buddy and I talked about."

"While I went for the car? I didn't think it was any of my business."

"All the old ghosts," she said.

It made sense but it didn't make sense. I waited.

"I lied to you. I was nervous about seeing him again."

I nodded.

"You don't spend as many years as I have, hating him and loving him, and not worry about the way you'll react when you meet him again." She used a hand to wipe the condensation away from the window next to her shoulder. "You know, his wife died in 1970."

"I saw the headstone."

"He still wants me," Rosemary said. "He asked if I'd divorce Charles and marry him."

"On a Sunday morning, in the church dining room?"

"It sounds silly, doesn't it?"

"No." My first inclination was to make fun of it. At the same time I knew I didn't have any right to influence it one way or the other. "No. It's just one of those human problems. He had to use what time he had. That particular time, that place."

She was silent until I pulled into my driveway and parked behind Hump's Buick. I cut the engine and waited.

"I said that it was too late for us. I said it might have been possible for us ten or twelve years ago. Not now. That there was too much dust and ashes and no fire." She hit the door handle and swung the door open. The misty rain blew in on us. "Does that please you, Jim?"

"It's nothing to me either way," I said.

"That's right." She stepped out. Before she closed the car door she turned back to me, laughing. "And you're no fun either."

Hump was planted in front of the TV set. It wasn't a football game. It was some old Alan Ladd movie. Hump waved a hand with a beer bottle in it. "Didn't expect you back so soon."

"We didn't stay for church."

I carried the grocery bag into the kitchen. Behind me, Hump switched off the TV set. He followed me into the kitchen and tossed his empty into the trash can. He leaned against the counter and watched me unload the bag. Rosemary draped her serape over a chair in the living room. She stopped in the kitchen doorway and nodded at the items on the table.

"Hump, do you know what this wild man is going to cook?"

"I'm working on it."

"Had lunch yet?" I said.

"I've been nibbling."

Hump put it together as soon as he saw the shrimp and the feta cheese. "Greek shrimp?"

I got the bottle of Graves from the pantry and placed it in the refrigerator.

Rosemary pulled back a chair and sat at the kitchen table. "What's Greek shrimp?"

"Mouthwatering," Hump said.

I left the bag of shrimp in the sink to thaw. I tried my pockets until I found the scrap of paper with Fred Thompson's address and phone number on it. "Did Art call?"

"Not yet." Hump opened two beers and passed one to me. "I guess he meant it about taking a Sunday rest from us."

On the way past I touched Rosemary on the shoulder. "I think I'd better call that lawyer friend of Buddy's."

"You need me?"

"Might be better if you make the call and put me on after the introductions."

She understood that. In the bedroom I pushed the covers aside and smoothed her a place on the bed near the night table. She sat on the edge of the bed and looked around. "Don't you ever make the bed, Jim?"

"And have to mess it up again every night?"

I dialed the number and passed the phone to Rosemary when I heard the first ring. I stood over her and waited.

"Mr. Thompson? This is Rosemary Atkinson. I'm Billie Joe's mother."

A pause. I could hear him talking.

"Of course, I can prove I'm Billie Joe's mother. What kind of question is that?"

I got Rosemary's attention and tapped myself on the chest. She nodded. "Mr. James Hardman, a friend who lives here in town, would like to talk to you."

I took the phone. Rosemary slid over and made room for me on the bed next to her. "I'm Jim Hardman. We just got back from Plainsville. Buddy gave us your name and address. We'd like to talk to you."

"If you're who you say you are ... you and the lady ... I'm still not certain what we have to talk about."

"About Billie Joe," I said.

"Is she back in Atlanta?"

"I don't think she ever left," I said.

There was a hissing, like breath passing his teeth. "Is that true?"

"It's true."

"I warned Buddy that seeing the girl was a mistake."

"That's old news, Mr. Thompson."

"You say you talked to Buddy today?"

I nudged my cuff back and checked my watch. "About two hours ago."

"I'll call you back."

"Huh?"

"I want to talk to Buddy."

"To check on us?"

"Yes," he said. "And what's your name again."

I gave him my name and phone number. He repeated the number and I said that was it.

"I think I've heard of you, Mr. Hardman."

"I was police a few years ago."

"You're the one," he said. "I'll call you." He broke the connection.

I replaced the receiver and stood up. "Even if I didn't know he was a lawyer, I could have guessed it. He's careful. Slow careful."

I filled my biggest pot with hot water from the tap. I dropped the bag of shrimp in. That would melt the ice frost away and continue the thawing. That was as much as I could do right away. I left them in the kitchen, Hump mixing her a scotch and water, and carried my beer into the bathroom. I washed up and drank part of the beer. On the way back through the bedroom, I thought about calling Art. I decided against it. He'd been firm about Sunday being his day of rest. Instead of that I made the bed and smoothed the wrinkles from the top blanket.

Crossing the living room I heard Hump say, "...the trip didn't do that much?"

"It didn't seem to," she said.

"Happens like that now and then," Hump said.

I had another swallow of beer before I found the large skillet and placed it on the burner. I lit the burner and let the skillet warm while I found the garlic press. When the skillet was warm, I turned off the burner and dropped in about a quarter stick of butter. The butter was melted by the time I had the tin of olive oil open. I mixed in three or four tablespoons of the oil.

"It that much of a blank in Plainsville, Jim?"

"Maybe." I broke off three large sections of garlic and peeled them. "The one thing I found out is that Billie Joe thinks she's a rebel with a cause."

"I can't believe that," Rosemary said.

"Whether you believe it or not doesn't count. It's what she believes." I pressed the three pieces of garlic over the skillet and scraped the pulp away. I put the burner on LOW and stirred the butter, the olive oil and the garlic while it simmered. "And it might fit. Who goes around robbing and shooting people? Leave out the cretins and the real criminals and what you've got left are the ones who think the world owes them something. That they've been shortchanged somehow."

I opened the can of tomatoes and poured the juice in. I chopped the tomatoes and stirred them into the sauce. A sprinkling of salt and pepper and a teaspoon of oregano that I rubbed together between my hands before I added it.

"Are you sure that's going to be eatable?" Rosemary asked Hump.

"You wait."

I left the sauce to simmer. I sat at the table, across from Rosemary. "Something's twisted, gone wrong, in these kids. I suspect they think they're the new outlaws. Apart from other people. Special. What applies to other people doesn't apply to them. Vague things have been done to them and they're going to collect. Dollars for wrongs."

"Billie Joe was brought up better than that."

"*Was* is the right word. Too much is boiling away inside her. What she thought of you, of Charles and Buddy. Anger and hurt, all stirred together and ladled up in iron against people who've never done anything to them. Like that woman at the 7–11."

"That's too much sociology for me," Hump said. "What they want is the easy money."

"Right to the heart of the matter," I said. I didn't believe that, but I felt silly doing all that talk, just trying to make Rosemary understand. It wasn't possible.

I got the bottle of wine from the refrigerator. It was barely chilled. I pulled the cork. According to the label it was a 1972 Clos de l'Eglise, whatever that meant. I poured about half a cup of the wine into the sauce and sniffed at it. It was getting right. "It's time Thompson called back."

I returned the wine to the refrigerator and went into the bedroom. Thompson's number was on the night table. I dialed it and waited through about eight rings. No answer.

Back in the kitchen, I shook my head before the question could be asked. "Out or not answering," I said.

"While we're waiting ..." Hump waved an arm at the skillet.

"Late lunch now or an early dinner in a couple of hours?"

"Now," Rosemary said.

"I'm with the lady."

I preheated the oven. The shrimp were still frozen to some degree. I drained them and dumped them into the sauce. I stirred them about until the clumps of two and three broke apart. By the time the sauce had overcome the chill of the shrimp and begun to bubble again, the oven was ready. I dampened the crusts of the sourdough bread and placed the loaves on the rack.

Rosemary set the table. The shallow soup bowls and wine glasses.

The shrimp curled and turned pink. I chopped the feta cheese into small cubes. The final touch: I dropped the feta into the sauce and waited until it started to melt.

"Ready." I stepped aside while Hump took the loaves of bread from the oven. Rosemary poured the Graves. I was ladling out the sauce and shrimp when the doorbell rang.

"Got it." Hump went to answer it.

Art Maloney said, "I was driving by, looking at the dogwoods."

"Come on back," Hump said.

Art stopped in the doorway. "That smells good, Jim. What is it?"

"Hungry?"

"I'll taste it."

I set out a bowl and a glass for him. When we were all served and seated, I broke off a big chunk of bread and said, "Eat the shrimp and dunk the sauce."

It was all the instruction they needed. The first few bites took the edge from my hunger. I nodded at Art. "How are the dogwoods?"

"That was a lie."

I knew it was. April and the blooming were still months away. "So what's the real reason for the visit?"

Art chewed and swallowed. "Curly and Shorty."

"Broke the case, huh?"

"Yesterday the word was *cracked*." He forked a shrimp into his mouth. "They still insist they don't know anything about Culp's killing. They just say they knew he was dead. Heard about it or read it in the paper."

I brought the skillet to the table and portioned out the rest of the sauce and shrimp. "You believe them?"

"Nothing ties them to it. Maybe they did it and maybe they didn't. If you've got any proof they did it, I'll be glad to take it home with me."

"Nothing," I said.

"That's it then." Art sopped a corner of bread in the sauce and chewed on it slowly. "Strange taste to this."

"That's the feta cheese," Hump said.

"And the wine," Rosemary said.

Art looked at Rosemary. "You didn't introduce me to this lady, Jim. Maybe you've got a good reason for it."

I did the introductions. "Sorry," I said, "but you came at the wrong time."

"I thought it was the right time." He nodded down at his bowl. "And I'm going to tell Marcy about this next time I see her."

"Tell her what?"

"That you've been cooking for strange ladies while she was out of town."

"I'm not strange, Mr. Maloney," Rosemary said.

Hump grinned, "Call him, Art."

"I'm not strange, Art."

"That's *strange* as in *stranger*," Art said. "No offense." He turned to me. "Funny thing about those bikers. After all that asking about Carl Culp, hours of it, they seemed willing to talk about anything else that came up. They seemed to welcome it. The girl you wanted me to ask them about ..."

"Billie Joe," I said. "Rosemary's daughter."

It was my way of warning him. I didn't know what he had to tell me. I wanted to hear it, but I'd put the tag on Billie Joe so that Art would cull any rough parts that might hurt Rosemary.

"They remember her all right. Culp brought her to a party."

"The same house?"

"Yeah."

"When was that?"

"Early September or late August. They're fuzzy about dates."

Whatever the date, it was probably after the trip she'd taken to Plainsville with her father. After the three or four days there before she broke with Buddy and returned to Atlanta.

"The party got rough. A lot of those biker parties do." He was picking his words and watching Rosemary out of the corner of his eyes. "The girl, Billie Joe, didn't want to play those games. She wanted to leave. Carl Culp got caught in the middle and roughed up. While that was going on, Billie Joe left."

"By herself?"

"The way they tell it," Art said. "It was funny to them. Laughed it up. Said her leaving was no great thing. Plenty of girls to go around. What they got their jollies on was that Culp came back a couple of days later. He said Billie Joe wouldn't see him anymore. She'd washed him out completely. That, after he'd taken his lumps protecting her."

"That all?" I ate the last shrimp and ran a crust of bread in the bowl until I'd wiped it clean of sauce.

"One bit more. Shorty said he had a yen for Billie Joe." Art's glance at Rosemary had an apology written in it. "The way Shorty saw it, if Billie Joe was through with Carl Culp, he might be able to interest her in something."

"He told you that ... out front?"

"I had to push him some. Anyway, he got Billie Joe's address from Culp and ..."

"Her address?" I looked at Hump.

"Sure. The apartment she was renting on Eighth Street."

"You got a number?"

"No."

"Damn."

"I tried for a number but he'd forgotten it. He says it was one of those renovated ones. Cream-colored stucco with a brown slat-like fence that fronts on the sidewalk."

"We might find it," Hump said.

"Art?"

"Yes, Rosemary?"

"What happened with Shorty and Rosemary?"

"She locked the door and said he'd better leave before she called the police."

"And ...?"

"He left. He said he believed that crazy broad meant it."

"Might be," I said to Hump. Then to Art: "You still holding those bikers?"

"Holding them for what? They've been out since yesterday."

I stood and drained my wine glass. "Hump and I have to take a ride."

"Eighth?" Art said.

"Before dark. So we can still see the colors. Do me a favor, Art."

"What favor?"

"Drop Rosemary at the Riviera."

"No, Jim." Rosemary moved around the table, clearing it. "I've got dishes to do. If I finish before you get back, I'll watch some TV." She was almost pleading. "I don't want to wait at the motel. I want to know what you find out."

I got my coat and returned to the kitchen. The dishes were stacked on the counter. She was running wash water in the sink. "If Fred Thompson calls ..."

"I'll say you'll call him back."

Art walked out front with us. The drive was full. He'd parked on the street. I touched his elbow and we stood in the thinning icy rain. "Anything important you left out in there?"

"About the bikers and Billie Joe?" Art shook his head. "All I left out was how rough the party games were."

"Thanks, Art."

Hump stood next to my Ford. "You try that cognac yet?"

"A sip," Art said. "It's too good to drink."

That was true. I was surprised that Art could taste the difference. I got a new look at Art. "It won't age in the bottle," I said.

I headed for the car. "Jim?"

"Yeah?"

"Ellison's been bitching about you around the department. He says you're mixing in police business."

Maybe it was the wine talking. I stuck a high finger as far in the air as I could. "That's for Ellison, wherever he is."

"Your funeral," Art said.

"And all my friends are invited."

CHAPTER NINE

One sweep up Eighth and one sweep back and we'd found the apartment house. In a stretch of three blocks, there were four walled and fenced-in buildings. One was green stucco, another was constructed out of brick and the third one was stone and mortar. The one we parked in front of appeared to be woven out of wooden slats. That gave it a rippled, waffled texture.

Past that wall, a breezeway ran the length of the apartments on the lower level. From the bank of mailboxes on the wall at the entrance to the breezeway, I estimated there were twenty or so units. I started at one side of the mailboxes. Hump started reading from the other side. Near the center, when I was about to say to hell with it, that we didn't know what we were looking for anyway, Hump said, "Look at this one."

His finger tapped a name card over the box for apartment number eight. The card, neatly typed, listed the tenant as Betsy M. Hart. Below her name, struck through with a double slash of a ballpoint pen, was B. J. James.

"Luck," I said.

"Or right living."

Apartment number eight was the final one on the left. The breezeway ended there, in an orderly row of the green garbage carts that the city had furnished a few months back. A red umbrella, closed and pointed downward, leaned against the right of the doorframe. A snake of water ran across the floor.

I pressed the bell button. I waited a minute and hit the button once more.

The door cracked a couple of inches. "What do you want?" It was a woman's voice, deep and throaty.

"I'm Jim Hardman. This is Hump Evans."

I could see one eye and a bit of red-blond hair. The eye was level with mine or almost there. "I don't know you." The door edged in, closing.

"Wait a minute. We're here about Billie Joe."

"That one?" The door opened to the limit of the chain. "What about her?"

"Who is it, Bet?" The voice was that of another woman. Her tone was softer, more feminine.

"Some men looking for a girl who used to live here."

"Look," I said, "we don't mean any harm. Could you talk to us for a few minutes?"

"About Billie Joe?"

"Yeah. Her mother's looking for her."

"Is she still lost?" A scrape of the lock and the chain was gone. "Wipe your feet on the way in." The door swung open.

I was right. She was a big one, this Betsy Hart. Five-eleven or so and built on the order of a Soviet lady shot-putter. Her hair was cut short and shaggy. A horsy face with freckles. Barefooted and barelegged in cut-off jeans. Broad-shouldered, she wore a gray tanktop without a bra under it. Heavy breasts jutted out, hardly moving when she walked.

I wiped my shoes on the thick mat. When I stepped from it, Hump followed me. I looked past Betsy Hart. A young girl, eighteen or nineteen, leaned against the doorway to the bedroom. Her dark hair was braided into a single pigtail. She wore a wine-red silk robe and was barelegged. She had on heavy wooden shower clogs.

Betsy Hart saw me look in her direction. Without turning, meeting my eyes, she said, "Take your shower, Jane. And close the door."

The living room was plain, without frills. The bedroom, the part I'd seen before Jane closed the door, was just as functional.

Both rooms looked like they belonged in the show apartment in a new housing development. Just what was needed. A dark red rug, a gray sofa, two rope-bottomed chairs and a glass-topped coffee table. There were no prints or paintings on the walls.

Betsy sat on the far end of the sofa. I sat in one rope-bottomed chair. Hump, when he was sure he'd scraped his shoes enough, sat in the other chair.

"I don't know why you'd want to talk to me. I haven't seen Billie Joe since the first week in October."

"How long did she stay here?"

"About a month. I think it was from the first part of September. She answered an advertisement I'd placed in the *Atlanta Gazette*. You know the kind of thing. Roommate wanted."

I nodded.

"She was a sweet little girl. Scared to death of life, if you know what I mean. Lord, the problems that girl had. And I can't help thinking most of them came from her mother."

"She talk about her mother a lot?"

"Enough," Betsy Hart said. "She called her mother the Dragonlady."

Hump leaned in and pulled an ashtray toward him. "What did she mean by that?"

"I'd rather you didn't smoke."

Hump put his smokes and matches away.

"What did she mean by Dragonlady?" She shrugged. "I think she meant that she could breathe fire. That she ate up people and chewed on the bones that were left."

"That's rough," I said.

"Often it's true."

"She only stayed here a month?" Hump got out a pack of mints and popped one in his mouth. He'd really wanted that smoke.

"It didn't work out well. It was only a matter of time."

"What was wrong?"

"I didn't mind that one boyfriend, Carl, being here at all hours. He seemed nice enough."

"Culp?"

She nodded. "But she gave him his walking papers. The rest of it was a nightmare."

"How?"

"She attracted a certain kind of man. Rough trade, I guess you could call them. A whole series of those. The last one, the soldier, was a bit much even for me."

I waited. I knew I didn't need to prompt her.

"It was the violence. The last straw was one Sunday night. They'd had a fight and she'd said she didn't want to see him anymore. He didn't accept that. He forced his way in. He was shouting and yelling and throwing furniture around. It was as if he thought he could force her, intimidate her, into caring about him again."

"You were here?"

"The whole time. When I'd had enough of it, I called the police. He went absolutely crazy then. He took a swing at me."

"Hit you?"

"No. I hit him. With a chair."

I believed her. She didn't look like anyone I'd want to duke it with.

"The police came about that time and took him away. He was charged with drunk and disorderly."

It wasn't much. It was good for maybe one night in jail.

"And you know what that silly little fool did? She bailed him out that same night. I'll tell you we had an argument about that. And that was it as far as her living here. The next day, while I was at work, she moved her belongings out."

"No good-bye?" I said.

"A note that blamed me for getting Bob in trouble."

"Bob's the soldier?"

She nodded. "I don't remember his last name."

The shower had been running in the other room. The rumble and row of it had become part of the atmosphere of the apartment. Now it ended and it seemed very quiet all of a sudden.

"This Bob, was he tall and thin with a white afro?"

"No. He was just the opposite of tall and thin. He was thick and heavyset with dark hair. A lot of greasy hair."

"Wear a ducktail?"

"Not then, but he was the type for it. I think the army must have made him cut it every month or two."

"He wear his uniform here?"

"Once or twice at the beginning. Then he wore civvies."

"What rank?"

"What?"

"How many stripes?"

"Two, I think. Maybe it was only one."

The bedroom door opened. The young girl, Jane, stopped in the doorway. She was wearing the robe and her hair was wrapped in a towel. I looked at her and I noticed that Betsy Hart was staring at me. It was the hard flat-eyed look.

"What is it, Jane?"

"Can I have a Coke?"

Betsy walked into the kitchen. While she was gone, Hump edged around and put his eyes on Jane. Jane gave him a bright, timid smile. The smile vanished when Betsy returned from the kitchen with the bottle of Coke. After she passed the Coke to Jane, Betsy gave her a gentle push that moved her into the bedroom. "We'll be done here in a minute." She pulled the door closed.

"Your new roommate?"

"A friend," she said. But she'd been reading me reading her and I got that same hard, flat look. The "go to hell. It's none of your business" look.

"The note was the last you heard from her?"

"Yes. And it was the last time I wanted to hear from her."

I dipped my head at Hump. He stood up.

"Appreciate you talking to us," he said. I followed him to the door. "Hated to bother you."

"One more thing," she said behind me. "That same week she left, another man came by looking for her."

"What kind of man?"

"Older. Expensively dressed. He seemed very upset that Billie Joe had moved out."

"Know who he was?"

"He said he was a friend of the family." Her tone of voice said that she didn't believe that.

"A sugar daddy?"

"That's the way I saw him."

I put my back to the door. "He give his name?"

"His name and his card," she said. "I threw the card away and I forgot his name."

"Describe him."

"About fifty. Maybe late forties instead. Neat gray hair. Tanned. The pinstripe-suit kind. A businessman, I think."

"Might be." I opened the door and turned.

"If you see her ..."

"Yes?"

"Tell her she owes me a month's rent, leaving that way."

In the car Hump grinned at me. "Different strokes."

I headed for home. Now that it was getting dark the rain was like hail on the windshield. The temperature was dropping. That would make for slick roads in the morning.

"The soldier got your attention?" Hump asked.

"The robbery I told you about. The one in the 7–11 when the woman was killed. The soldier, Bob, might be the one with the stack of cat-food cans."

"Got a way to find him?"

"I'll think of one." I already had.

Half a block from my house, Hump said, "Don't turn in the drive. I'll back out first."

"How about a drink?"

"Not tonight. There's this bit of trim I might stop by and bless."

I braked on the road. "You can drop Rosemary at her motel on your way."

Hump put a hand on the door handle. "You're one dumb man, Hardman."

"What's that supposed to mean?"

"You know damned well."

I guess I did. I'd spent the whole day trying to walk around it. Maybe if I got a look at the back of it, it would disappear.

"See you tomorrow." Hump swung the door open and stepped out. I waited while he backed his Buick out of the driveway and into the road. As I pulled past him, he honked his horn at me.

It sounded like his shave-and-a- haircut honk.

I edited it the best I could. I left out the Dragonlady remark. I changed Betsy Hart into a nice older lady who'd taken good care of Billie Joe. When I got done with her, you'd have thought she was a spinster lady who taught Sunday school.

There wasn't much I could do with the soldier boy, Bob.

Rosemary took it well. Better than I'd expected her to. That might have been the booze. While we were away, the level of the scotch had gone down a couple or three inches.

I had a beer while we talked. After that I switched to coffee and cognac. It was the right time for brandy. The icy rain beat on the window like somebody tapping it with a pencil tip. It was a nasty night out.

The TV movie listed for the night was one of those three-hour spaghetti Westerns made in Spain. It starred some gay American actor. By ten-thirty I'd had too much brandy and I'd lost interest in the flick. It was an absurd bloodbath. The hero was killing people with a six-gun that fired rounds almost as big as antitank shells.

I yawned at Rosemary. She'd taken off her boots and curled up on the sofa with a drink on her stomach. "Time to go," I said. She didn't answer. I went into the bedroom and got my topcoat. When I came back, she was sitting up. She hadn't put on her boots yet.

"I owe you for a phone call," she said. "I called Charles so he'd know everything was fine."

"Is everything fine?" I yawned again. "Don't worry about the call."

"Jim?" Her voice was soft, slurred by the scotch.

"Huh?"

"Let me sleep on the sofa tonight."

"I don't know," I said. "That might make problems."

"I promise I won't attack you."

"I didn't think you would."

"Didn't you?" Her laugh had all the strings pulled loose.

"You still got the motel room blues?"

She nodded.

"The bed's yours."

"No, Jim."

"Either that," I said, "or I'll call a cab for you."

"Is something wrong with your car?"

"Something's wrong with me." I yawned and rubbed my eyes. "I'm drunk tired."

"All right, Jim."

I got to my feet and wobbled to the bedroom. I found clean sheets and a pillowcase. I hadn't heard her but when I turned she was behind me. She took the linen and said, "I'll change the bed."

I left her to that and took pajamas and a robe into the bathroom. After a wash, I changed into the p.j.'s and the robe. On the way through the bedroom, I saw that the bed was made. It was neat, without a wrinkle. I stopped in the doorway. "You bring anything to sleep in?"

"I hadn't planned to stay."

In the back of one of the dresser drawers I found a blue flannel shirt that I'd bought a winter before. The sleeves were too long for me and I hadn't worn it but a time or two. I removed the plastic collar stays and placed it next to the pillow.

I sipped a final cognac while we watched the last of the movie. Time ran slow and rough, as if somebody had replaced the sand in the hourglass with pebbles. If I was going to make a move, if she expected it, it was time. If I wasn't, it was past time.

"Time for bed," I said.

That was strong decision-making for you.

I was dreaming. I thought I was dreaming. In the dream I could smell her scent, her perfume or cologne. That's all right, I told myself. The whole house is full of her special smell. It will take a week of garlic and armpits to rid this room of her. Nothing to it. Or it is a sense memory. Trapped far back in my nostrils, there for a month or a year.

"Jim." Soft, her voice, but a child's voice.

I opened my eyes. I hadn't spread the sofa. I was sleeping on the narrow length of it, face pressed into the scratchy fabric of the back. I rolled over.

The bedroom lamp backlighted her. Naked, she stood over me. The front of her was dark in shadows. The outline of her glowed, a photo burning from the corners inward.

"I can't sleep, Jim. Help me sleep."

I tried to move my tongue. It was heavy and I could feel raw cracks in it. Someone had been stropping a straight razor on it. That was the cognac.

She sat on the sofa next to me, nudging me with her hip so that I'd make room for her. "Jim…"

My tongue could move after all. "The other people…"

"This has nothing to do with Charles."

"There's Marcy …"

"And it doesn't have anything to do with Marcy either." One of her hands moved over my chest, ruffling the hair and warming the skin. "This concerns you and me and nobody else."

"Us," I said.

"That's right."

She leaned forward and her hair fell across my face. Her mouth was hard. The taste of garlic and old scotch. Tongue searching my hurt tongue until my mouth was full of pain.

It was over and it had just begun.

CHAPTER TEN

I t wasn't perfume. It was something else. I came up out of the darkness and breathed in, clearing my nose. That was it. It was the scent of bacon and eggs.

I sat up and wished I hadn't. My head felt like a shattered tooth. I sat on the edge of the bed, head down, until I thought the chances were about fifty-fifty that I could stand without falling down. That view of the room revealed an ashtray that had been knocked off the coffee table, the butts and the ashes scattered in a line so that it looked like a comet with a tail. The blue flannel shirt I'd loaned Rosemary for a nightgown was on the floor next to the bedroom door.

Thigh and groin tired. I eased to my feet. My pajamas were strung over the back of the easy chair. I struggled into them and wobbled into the kitchen. I found Rosemary having her breakfast. She was dressed in the pants suit from the day before. She'd made herself up and her hair was neat, carefully groomed.

"I thought I'd let you sleep, Jim."

"It's a good thought. I can't. I've got things to do." I met her eyes. Hers slid away. That was the way it was. Last night was last night and today was today. I'd never learned how to deal with the mornings after anyway.

"I'll fix you some breakfast."

"Coffee to start with," I said, "until I see what my stomach thinks of it. I've got some calls to make." I had my look at the kitchen wall clock. It was 9:23.

I left her making the coffee. In the bathroom I ran some water and dunked my face in it. I wrapped a towel around my neck and went into the bedroom. I sat on the edge of the bed and dialed Hump's number.

"I think I'm getting a cold," he said. "It was all that mushing about in bad weather."

"You coming over?"

"I thought I'd wait for an invitation."

"You've got it."

"You want me to pick up Rosemary at the Riviera?"

"She's already here," I said.

He laughed and broke the connection.

The second call was to Art Maloney.

"Screw you, Jim. The answer is no."

"I need a meet with Ellison. I want you to referee it for me."

"What's in it for him?"

"I might be able to ID one of those boys who killed the woman at the 7–11 last Wednesday."

"That might grab him," Art said. "What's in it for you?"

"Brown points. Enough of them so that he might leave me alone."

"Don't bet on it. You at home?"

"I am until I hear from you."

"Stay there. I'll call you or we'll come by. One or the other."

I put the phone down and dry-heaved into the towel.

I shaved and showered and dressed. For show to Ellison, I picked out a good pair of dark brown trousers and my good tweed jacket. By the time I reached the kitchen, the dishes were washed and draining and the coffee she'd mixed me was cool. I drank it anyway and made myself a second cup. Rosemary watched me over the women's section of the *Constitution*.

"Hump's on his way."

That wasn't what she'd primed herself to talk about. "Last night, Jim …"

I'd prepared myself too. "Talking spoils it. It was just one of those human situations."

"You're a funny man."

"Oh, yes," I said.

"And a nice one too."

I carried my cup to the table and sat down across from her. "If I can't be beautiful, I'd rather be nice. That was what my mama told me to do."

"Now you're not being funny." Level, serious eyes.

"It's my head. It feels like a garbage bag full of rocks and broken bottles. It clanks and rattles."

"That's funny."

I shook my head. The dizziness blurred my eyes. "Small talk for mornings after."

I hadn't heard Hump drive up. He walked around the house and knocked at the back door. He let himself in after a short wait. "Lord, it's slick out there." He shucked his coat and carried it to the living room doorway. I saw him hesitate when he saw the bed linen and the blanket on the sofa. He tossed his coat over the back of the easy chair. "You two look serious."

"I tried to drink all the brandy in the house."

Rosemary smiled. "I tried to match him with the scotch."

"Good reasons," Hump said. "Got some coffee?"

While Rosemary fixed him a cup, Hump sat across from me. The question was on his face. I pretended not to see it. I told him about the call to Art.

"Soldier boy?"

I nodded. Rosemary passed the coffee to him and left the kitchen. Past Hump I could see her moving back and forth in the living room, straightening up. Hump still had the question on his face. It was going to be there all day. I nodded and shrugged. That said it all. Yes and confusion.

The knowing grin had started. It faded. It was back to business. "You think Ellison will buy it?"

"I would." I lit a smoke and felt the heat burning the cut places on my tongue. I stubbed it out. "A good cop always takes the help of a good citizen."

At the doorway Rosemary worked her head through the yoke of the serape. "I need to call a cab. I've got to go back to the motel."

I stood up. Hump shook his head at me. "You've got to stay here, Jim. I'll drive her." He gulped his coffee.

I followed them to the door and touched Rosemary on the shoulder. "So much was happening yesterday I didn't ask. Did Fred Thompson call back?"

"No."

I watched them drive away, toward town. It was bitter cold. There was ice on my steps, ice coating the winter brown grass on my lawn.

"The coffee's still rotten." Ellison said.

"So don't drink it." I said.

Art stared down into his cup. Some referee. He'd hardly said a word since they'd arrived. Ellison...I still hadn't heard his first name...sat next to him on the sofa. Ellison looked like he'd just come off night duty. He needed a shave and his eyes were red-rimmed.

"All this small talk aside, I got pushed into this by Maloney. If it was up to me, you could whistle for breath."

Art lifted his head. "Listen him out."

"I said I would."

"Bitch about it later then." Art turned on me to soften it. "And this better be worth our time, Jim."

"Got a pencil?"

Ellison flipped his notebook open and uncapped a felt-tipped pen.

"The first week in October, Billie Joe James was sharing an apartment with a woman named Betsy Hart on Eighth Street." I searched my head and found the street number and read it off for them. I stared at Ellison until he shrugged and noted it. "She was going at the time with a guy named Bob ... Bob something."

"Is that all you know?"

"Let me finish. A Sunday that first week in October the dude, Bob, caused some trouble at the apartment and got hauled off by the police. Drunk and disorderly."

It was a tennis match. I flipped back and forth from the faces. Art was interested but he was puzzled. "Get to the bottom line, Jim."

"That's most of it. Except for the fact ..." I let it trail away. I faced Ellison. "Remember the night at the 7–11? I told you one of the guys there had taken some cans of cat food?"

"It was a lot of help," Ellison said.

"The description the Hart woman gives of this Bob something dude comes close to matching the guy in the 7–11, the one with the cat food."

Ellison did a quick sweep of the room with his eyes.

"The phone's in the bedroom." I waved an arm in that direction. I waited until he reached the doorway. "One more thing that might help. This Bob wore a uniform part of the time. Army."

"Then the M.P.s would have picked him up at the slammer."

"If they'd known he was a soldier. What I hear is that Billie Joe bailed him out that same night. He was wearing civvies."

Ellison reached the foot of the bed before he turned and slammed the bedroom door.

"He's young," Art said.

"He's aging slow," I said. I carried my cup into the kitchen and left it on the table. "And you're some referee."

"I got him here. It wasn't easy. I had to lie and say that you'd been a half-decent cop at one time."

"High praise from you."

"He didn't buy any part of it."

After five or six minutes Ellison opened the bedroom door. "It smells like a whorehouse in there."

"You must go to the good ones. That stuff's probably fifty an ounce."

"Get on with it," Art said. He was tired of the bickering.

"The last name's Buchner. Robert Bruce Buchner. He didn't show for court. He forfeited bail." He looked at me. "And you were right. Billie Joe James put up the bail money."

"A home address from the arrest sheet?"

"Yeah." He didn't read it.

"Make the other call?"

"Fort Mac says he's been A.W.O.L. since that weekend. A couple of weeks ago the time ran out and they turned it over to the F.B.I."

"Photo?"

"I think we can get one from the Bureau." Ellison picked up a plaid topcoat and put it on. "A cruiser will meet us there."

I got my coat and followed them to the door. Ellison turned and blocked my way. "Where you think you're going?"

"I thought I'd stay with you until you said thanks."

"You'll get a letter." He dropped his arm. "It'll have a fancy letterhead."

"You might need an on-the-spot ID of the kid."

"Just for the ride?" Art said.

"Me get involved with gunplay?"

Ellison agreed. "He's your problem."

Hump pulled into the driveway as we came down the front steps. He gave the two unmarked cars on the street a puzzled look. Ellison and Art cut across the lawn to their cars. I made a wide circle and met Hump on the walk. "The back door is open."

"I come with you?"

"They don't even want me along."

Art honked. I trotted across the icy lawn and got into the car with him.

We tailgated Ellison. When Ellison turned onto Argonne a possibility hit me. I didn't really believe it until I saw the police cruiser parked next to the big frame house painted battleship gray. "I think Hump's been here."

"Huh?" He was concentrating on house numbers.

"Nothing."

We parked one house down. Ellison was out of his car quickly. Two uniformed cops got out of the cruiser and met him. One of the cops looked about my age and he was about as over-weight as I am. The other was younger, probably in his first year on the force. The older cop carried the riot gun.

It was settled by the time Art and I reached them. Ellison pointed at me. "You stay out here. Any ID needs making can be done later." I leaned against a telephone pole. The four of them headed up the walk. About halfway there, Ellison tapped the fat, older cop on the shoulder. He said something I didn't hear. The fat cop waddled back and stood next to me, the riot gun at port arms.

"I'm just a witness," I said.

"He didn't say that."

"What'd he say?"

"He said to stay with you." His arms got tired. He lowered the riot gun and eased the butt to the sidewalk. "You sure you're not involved in this?"

"Me? That's an insult."

He belched, a low, controlled rumble. Breakfast sausage probably.

The front door closed behind the other three. I got out my smokes and lit one. A couple of puffs and I heard another rumble. It wasn't the fat cop. This rumble had a squeak mixed in it. It came from the driveway to the left of the apartment house. I looked in that direction and after a few seconds one of those green garbage carts appeared past the corner of the house. A tall man with a wide-brimmed leather hat was pushing it. He had his head down.

"You got another one of those?" The cop indicated my cigarette.

I dug out my pack and shook out one for him. He braced the riot gun between his knees and lit it with his own matches. It took him three matches, the wind was that bad. After a short draw or two he cupped his hand around it, as if to hide it. "Thanks."

I looked over my shoulder, toward the corner of Fifth and Argonne. It took me a count of ten before it sank in. I looked quickly in the other direction, toward Ponce de Leon. The same. There weren't any other garbage carts at the curbs. Strange. Most collection days the curbs are loaded.

The tall man in the leather hat stepped away from the garbage cart and made an elaborate gesture of brushing his hands on his jeans. Then he turned and walked in the direction of Ponce de Leon, away from the fat cop and me.

It was partly the solitary garbage cart. It was partly a hunch. I stepped around the fat cop and yelled, "Hey, you." The tall man whirled and I got a brief look at his face. It didn't mean much until he jerked the hat from his head. That was to keep it from falling off when he ran. And run he did. But not before I put the face and the white afro together and knew that this was the other young man from the 7–11 robbery and murder.

The fat cop said, "What the hell?" He grabbed at my arm. I shook him away. I lurched into a run. Behind me the cop said, "Stop. Hey, you, stop."

I heard a round pumped into the riot gun.

Oh, shit. I kept running. Ahead of me, the tall man swerved and sprinted into the street, heading for the other side. Behind me, the cop yelled, "Stop or I'll fire."

I couldn't stop. My head was telling me to but my legs kept moving. The man in front of me was running smoothly, almost gliding. As he ran the leather hat flopped in his left hand. He reached the other sidewalk and his right hand was digging at his waistband. His hand came out holding iron. Something short-barreled.

The fat cop was chasing me. Heavy feet pounding right behind me. I ran into the street. He was close. I shouted over my shoulder. "Him ... him ... he's one of them."

"One of who?" His face was chalk-white. He looked about a breath away from a heart attack.

"Them."

He was close enough to swing the butt of the riot gun at me. I dodged away from it.

"Stop that, goddammit."

I looked for the tall man. He was standing at the base of a driveway. He brought the gun up, aiming. A battered white van was parked next to the other curb. I put my hands over my head and made a dive for it as cover. I heard the skin tearing from my elbows and knees. I skidded until I was against the rear left tire. The fat cop finally understood. He saw the gun and made his dive. He landed half on me and half on the riot gun.

The tall boy fired. The round broke the rear window of the van. I gave the fat cop a shove and pushed him off me.

More running and shouting. Art, Ellison and the young cop were running toward us. I had my look past the tire and saw that the driveway was empty. I stood and looked at the fat cop. He was holding his ribs, pain on his face. I leaned over him and picked up the riot gun.

I was winded. The four of us reached the base of the drive at the same time. Ellison waved an arm at the young cop. "Take the cruiser. Cover the back side of this street."

The young cop sprinted away. He passed the fat cop who was leaning against the van, holding on to a luggage rack on top. He shouted something at the young cop. The cop ignored him and sprinted past.

Ellison looked at the riot gun. "Where'd you get that?"

"Your man dropped it."

He jerked it out of my hands.

"There's a round in the chamber."

Art gestured up the drive. "He the other one?"

"White afro," I said.

A distance apart, they moved up the driveway abreast. I tagged behind. At the head of it, blocking the way, was an old wooden garage with high double doors. To the right there was a backyard and a low fence. Beyond that there was another yard and the back of a house that fronted one street over. To the left, bordering the drive, was a high brick wall that closed off the yard to the next-door house. The wall was about seven feet high.

The wall was on Ellison's side. He placed the riot gun on the top of the wall and pulled himself up to peer over it. Art swung to the right and checked the yard. He went as far as the low fence before he turned and came back.

I watched them. I moved up the middle of the drive until I was a couple of feet from the garage front. Both doors were pulled in tight. I stopped and looked down. In front of the right hand door there was a fanlike scrape in the patch of ice. I backed away.

Art backed his way to the drive. I met him and put a finger to my mouth. I pointed to the scrape in the ice. He edged toward it, squatted and backed away.

Ellison lowered himself from the wall. "Nothing over there."

Art pointed at the garage.

"Put a round in there," I said.

"Who the hell do you think you're …?"

"Do it," Art said.

"It's on your head." Ellison put the riot gun to his shoulder. I could see from the angle that he was aiming high. When the round hit the doors it blew off the top right corner of the left door.

"Throw the iron out." I'd waited until I could hear again before I yelled. I wanted to be certain he'd hear me.

"Do it," Art said. "You're boxed."

"Another round," I said. "This time knee-high."

"Wait." The boy's voice sounded muffled.

The right door moved outward. The ice patch squeaked. A few seconds later he tossed out the gun. It skidded down the slope of the drive and stopped at my feet.

CHAPTER ELEVEN

The apartment was on the second floor of the three-story building. Three was a narrow dark hallway with an exit at the rear. Number seven was near the exit, at the back of the floor. The two windows looked out on to the driveway and into the shuttered windows of the house next door. As soon as I had my look out the windows, I left Art and Ellison questioning the kid and walked down the hall to the exit. There was a straight-down flight of wooden stairs that led to the backyard. Against the back wall of the building, numbers painted on the top covers, were the green garbage carts. The cart for number seven was missing.

I could smell the apartment even before I entered it. The smell of cooking grease, dirty socks and sweat and a couple of other bad odors that I couldn't separate from the mixture.

It was essentially one big room. An unmade queen-sized bed was placed to the right, the length of it against the wall. Beyond the bed there was a door that led into a bathroom. Straight ahead, through a narrow doorway, there was a closet of a kitchen and dining room.

Hands cuffed behind him, the kid sat on the edge of the bed. He still had the leather hat on. He'd been wearing it when he came out of the garage across the street. Art was next to the window, warming his hands on the old steam radiator. Ellison stood in front of the boy, wide-legged and menacing.

"... fat man places you at the 7–11 on the seventeenth. That's murder one whether you pulled the trigger or not."

"What fat man?"

Art rubbed his hands together and shook his head at me. That meant, stay out of it.

Ellison ignored me. "You going to take the whole rap yourself, Brian?"

That was his name. Brian Case. We'd gotten it from the driver's license in his wallet. He'd turned eighteen back in the summer. Just past being a juvenile. Old enough to burn if they still burned people.

Brian looked past Ellison. He was either bored or disinterested.

I settled my rump on the radiator. "He's a tough one," I said. "Or a smart one."

Ellison spun on me. I had the edge on him. I'd already started. It would take the sting out of it if we argued among ourselves. I went on with it. "He knows there's no capital punishment anymore. Even if the slug matches the one that killed the woman clerk, all he'll do is time." I turned to Art. "How much?"

"Fifteen years before he see his first parole board."

"That's not bad. If he makes it past the board his first time, he won't even be forty by the time he's on the street again."

"He's smart all right," Art said.

"Of course, by then, the hard-asses in there'll have him wearing lipstick and eye shadow and perfume."

"Perfume's hard to get in there," Art said. "Some of the chicks have to make do with vanilla extract."

"Not Brian here. He'll have friends outside. They'll ship him Max Factor sets on Christmas and his birthday."

"Good to have friends you can depend on," Ellison said. He'd joined in, I thought, because he saw that we were getting to the boy. Most men had their own special nightmares. The one that many of the straight ones have about prison is homosexual rape. That aspect hadn't been a part of the prison atmosphere we got from the Cagney or the Bogart films. Lately the papers and the television reports were full of it.

"Those friends?" I shook my head.

"Bob Buchner and Billie Joe? You think they wouldn't take care of a friend?" Ellison stared down at Brian. "That's right. We know their names."

"I never heard of either of them," the boy said.

I pushed away from the radiator before I got burn stripes. There was a closet to the left of the bed. I opened the door and found a pull cord for the light. There wasn't much inside. Some shirts, a couple of sweaters, an old leather flight jacket with the leather peeling away. Some jeans. I pushed those aside and found a blue granny dress in a flower print. "All three of you live here together?"

"Share the same bed?" Art asked.

"That must be fun and games." Ellison leaned past the boy and had a look at the dress.

"I don't live here," Brian said.

"When's garbage pickup over here?"

Ellison stared at me like he thought I'd gone crazy.

"Tomorrow morning," the boy said.

I heard a scratching under the bed. An orange tabby with one cropped ear strolled from under the bed. It looked at us and didn't seem to be bothered at all. It stretched and yawned.

That was one of the smells I hadn't been able to isolate from the others. I closed the closet and went into the kitchen. There was a plastic dishpan on the kitchen floor with kitty litter in it that needed changing. Near it was a dish of dry food and a water saucer. Another saucer held the remainder of a freshly opened can of cat food.

"That's it," I said. "Brian's doing his friendly. He's feeding the cat for Bob and Billie Joe." While I stood in the kitchen door, the tabby brushed against my leg and swaggered to the dry food. The crunch-crunch started. "Let me make another guess. Bob and Billie Joe went out of town and didn't ask Brian along. Every day he comes over here and feeds the cat. And today he put out the garbage cart because he won't be back until tomorrow afternoon and the trucks will have gone by then." That also explained something that I hadn't understood. How the boy could have known that we were coming after him. He couldn't have seen us from the window. It was, instead, a matter of bad timing. He'd fed the cat and was on his way out when he saw me and the fat cop in front.

"Fuck you, fat man," the boy said.

"See? He can talk."

"Robbers take vacations just like everybody else," Art said. "Especially at Christmas."

Ellison gave the apartment a last long look. "We done here?"

Art said he was.

Art switched off the lights. Ellison closed the door and checked to see that it locked. Brian wagged his head toward the door. "What about Charlie?"

"Charlie's the cat?"

"Yeah."

"We'll send somebody over to feed him." Ellison took Brian by the elbow and turned him toward the stairs. "He won't be lonely."

The wagon was on the way. Ellison stopped Brian on the front stairs and seated him on the bottom step. The boy tilted his head back. The brim of the leather hat flopped over his eyes.

"I want to call my lawyer."

"You got a lawyer?" Ellison unwrapped a stick of Juicy Fruit, rolled it up and popped it into his mouth.

"I know the name of one."

"You make your call from the station," Ellison said.

Art and I walked a few paces away from the steps. Art was relaxed now and pleasant enough. It was a good collar. The first of three wanted for murder and Lord knows how many robberies. Not that the collar would do Art much good. There were too many years of not playing politics right. He'd broken a few balls here and there and I thought he was probably red-lined, about as far as he could go. But there wasn't a better cop on the force and even the people he gave the red-ass knew it.

"How many browns did I pick up?"

"I haven't done a count yet, Jim."

"You think Ellison will thank me before he leaves?"

"You trying to hustle a bet with me?"

At the steps, Ellison tapped the boy on the shoulder. "Don't move. You run and I'll put a hole in you that you couldn't plug with a roll of paper towels."

"I ain't going anywhere."

Ellison walked over to us and turned, his eyes on the boy. "I guess we can assume that this was a positive ID, Hardman."

"Maybe," I said. "Maybe not."

"What the fuck does that mean?"

"That clown of yours almost put a hole in me."

"A mistake," Ellison said.

"That's easy enough for you to say. It wasn't your hide he was aiming at."

"What's that got to do with whether you'll do a positive ID on the boy?"

"Not much," I said. "But I've got to consider my reputation."

"What reputation?"

"That's it. The one I've got with you people. The one that people buy and sell my ass for small change."

"It's that one you earned yourself," he said.

"In that case, since that's supposed to be true, maybe I ought to wait and talk to the kid's lawyer. Maybe I can sell him my memory."

"Goddammit, you two." It was about as loud as I've ever heard Art shout. "You two shut up."

"The hell I will." I got out a smoke, but my hand was shaking so much with the anger that I knew I'd never get it lit. I broke the cigarette shoving it back in the pack. "I pointed this one for you.

And I ran him down while you two were upstairs checking the sheets for sperm tracks. And I almost got shot in the butt by one of Atlanta's fat finest while doing it. All that, I think, makes me a pretty damned good bird dog."

"What is it you want, Jim?"

The paddy wagon was a block away, heading in from Ponce de Leon.

"I want what every good bird dog gets. A pat on the head."

"Oh, hell." Art leaned toward me and tapped me on the top of my head with an open palm. It was as much a slap as a pat.

I looked at Ellison. He'd almost swallowed his stick of gum. "Is that all you want, Hardman? I thought it was something important."

Eyeball to eyeball with him. "It is."

"All right." It was given grudgingly. "Good work, Mr. Hardman. And thanks a lot."

I grinned at both of them. "You just made my day. I'm so happy I might pee on myself."

Art dropped me at my place. He had little to say during the drive. He parked on the street and waited until I was halfway out of the car before he threw his head back and laughed. It was a real belly laugh; something had been bottled and shook, waiting for the cap to come off.

"Jim," he sputtered at me, "that was the most outrageous shit I've ever seen."

"What?" I gave him my bland face.

"The shit you pulled on Ellison."

"Just on Ellison?" I laughed with him. "Wasn't it fun, though?"

I limped into the house. Now that I'd cooled I could feel the scratches and scrapes. It was hell to get old and still find yourself playing cowboys and Indians.

Hump was in the kitchen. I asked him to bring me a beer. I undressed down to my underwear and took the beer when he came to the doorway. I sat on the bed and inspected my knees. One looked bad enough so that it would probably scab up. Both elbows were missing skin.

The elbows caught Hump's attention. "I wasn't sure you still had it, old man."

"I don't."

"Like this girl said to me once, a gentleman rests on his elbows."

"Huh?"

"Balling."

"Oh." I got up and limped toward the bathroom. "This wasn't any rest. I was ass saving." I washed my knees and elbows with soap and water and took the bottle of iodine from the medicine cabinet. When I returned to the bedroom, I had red elbows and knees.

"All that interest in how your night went almost made me forget."

"What?"

"That lawyer, Fred Thompson, called. He said he was ready to talk to you. I told him to drop by." He glanced at his watch. "He said he'd come by at one. Twenty minutes from now."

"I'm not sure we need to see him. We might have gone past that."

I dressed. By the time we'd moved to the kitchen and I'd made myself a cheese sandwich, I'd told him about the morning.

"Rosemary will want to know about this."

"You call her," I said.

"Some problem?"

"Might be. My guess is, when Bob Buchner and Billie Joe come back from their vacation, they're going to find that house staked out. Guns enough there to start a banana war or two. That girl don't play it right, she might get her butt blown away."

"Now that I understand, boss man, you make the call."

"Flip you for it."

The phone rang in the bedroom. Hump said, "I don't hear any phone."

I had to take the call. It was a woman but it wasn't Rosemary. "This is Mr. Thompson's secretary."

"Jim Hardman," I said.

"Mr. Thompson asked me to tell you that he has been called out of the office on business. He will call you later and reschedule your appointment with him."

A hunch, a lowdown, far-out hunch. "Maybe I could reach him at the police station."

"I'm not at liberty to say..." She broke off, paused and tried again. "I don't know where you can reach him, Mr. Hardman."

Good try but no cigar, lady. "Thanks, anyway."

I hung up and went back into the kitchen. Hell, I told myself, there's nothing to hang that on. No peg, no nail. With the crime rate what it is, maybe twenty people might have been arrested in the last few hours. And there must be others in there who hadn't made bail over the weekend and were just finding themselves a lawyer.

It nagged at me. Still, it was too stupid to mention to Hump. I walked around it, circling it like a tired fighter, and then I went back to the phone and called Ellison.

Ellison said, yes, the kid had called his lawyer. No, he hadn't listened to the call and he didn't know which lawyer the kid had contacted.

I said, "How about trusting me for a minute and finding out what lawyer shows up to see Brian."

He said he would.

He called back in fifteen minutes.

CHAPTER TWELVE

red Thompson's law office was in a low glass-fronted building that had been a florist shop a few years back. I think I remember having stopped there once to buy yellow roses for Marcy. Now they'd put up some kind of metallic brown drapes and installed an ornate heavy wooden door. It was located on West Peachtree between Twelfth and Thirteenth.

We were parked across the street in the lot next to The Garden Spot, a store that specialized in plants and pots and such. I was in Art's car with Betsy Hart. She filled the center of the front seat, pressing Art against one door and me against the other one. It had been some trouble finding Betsy. It had taken most of an hour to find where she worked and collect her from the ad agency. The resident manager had been helpful when we'd started the trace at the apartment house on Eighth.

We'd been in the parking lot since 4:15. It was cold, and every few minutes Art would run the engine for a few minutes so the heater would kick in.

Hump was parked next to us in his Buick.

At one minute after five, the secretary came out of the office. Art passed Betsy a pair of binoculars and said, "Focus them on her." The secretary was bundled in a scarf and a knit hat. It was lucky we weren't trying to identify her. All I could see of her was her nose.

She drove away in a tan Pinto. That left a black Continental in the last space to the far right.

"Got it?"

Betsy nodded and lowered the binoculars. It was five minutes before the heavy door opened again. This time it was a gray-haired man in a black or blue-black topcoat. He locked the door and turned and stood that way for a few seconds before he lifted a dark hat with a gray band and placed it on his head.

I watched Betsy Hart track him to the Continental.

"What do you think?" I had a hand on the door handle.

"He's the man." She lowered the binoculars and passed them to Art. "He came to the apartment two or three days after Billie Joe moved out."

I swung the passenger door open. "Thanks. Mr. Maloney will drop you at your office." Across the street, Thompson had started the Continental. He was warming the engine.

"Jim .. . ?" Art had some questions.

I didn't have time. "I'll call soon as I can." I slammed the door and trotted around the back of Hump's Buick. He had the door open for me. The engine was running. "The lady says that's the sugar daddy."

The Continental found a hole in the rush-hour traffic and slipped into it. Thompson was headed for the higher numbers, toward Peachtree Road.

Hump butted into the traffic three cars back and we followed.

It had been a dumb argument. Art knew it and I knew it. It was all I could do to keep from laughing. Dumb, dumb, double dumb.

"Look at it this way, Art. Thompson tells the girl's daddy he dropped her at the bus station the first week in September and pointed her toward Kingstree. If I'm right, if the sugar-daddy type is Fred Thompson, he was lying. He knew the whole time that Billie Joe didn't leave Atlanta. One month after he's supposed to have shipped her out of town he's at the apartment on Eighth asking about her."

"Weak," Art had said. "You know how many men there are in Atlanta with gray hair, in the age range from late forties to early fifties?"

"Thousands."

"Many thousands."

"All right. But we pick up Brian Case somewhere around noon. It just happens the lawyer he calls is Fred Thompson?"

"That's a hell of a leap."

"Not if Thompson is the sugar daddy Betsy Hart saw."

"Even then," Art said, "what have you got?"

"Too big a knot." It was the frustration of grabbing at wispy things. "Look, I called him after Rosemary and I got back from Plainsville. He says he'll call Buddy and call us back. He doesn't. I call him and he's not there."

"Or he's there and he doesn't answer."

"I think I flushed him. No phone in that apartment on Argonne, was there? I think he drove to the apartment to tell Billie Joe her mother and I were asking about her. He didn't find her. That was yesterday. Now, today, he talked to Brian Case at the slammer. He has to know that the place on Argonne is being watched. The town is heating up. If he knows how to reach her, he's probably warned her. If he doesn't know, then he has to find a way to shortstop her. Either way he's probably going to contact her." I stopped and took a deep breath. "I think it's worth a day or two of watch and follow."

"If he's the right gray-haired man."

"Yeah."

That was when we drove to Eighth and asked our question about Betsy Hart.

Oddly, in the heavy homeward traffic, there was less chance to lose him than in light traffic. Once you got in one lane you were locked in, nailed down.

Hump cruised two cars back.

Straight out Peachtree Road. Past Brookwood Station. Past Piedmont Hospital.

"Where the hell's he going?"

"Home," I said.

Home for Fred Thompson was a condominium in the Farr Hills development. It looked like twenty or so units with another ten or so framed out and underway. We passed under a gray brick archway that had FARR HILL, in wrought iron, dangling, swinging in the wind. All the condominiums were constructed from dark wood that wasn't painted. It was supposed to weather, I think. It reminded me of houses I'd seen in rural parts of Japan. There, for whatever reason, the wood aged, weathered, until it was like driftwood.

The Continental swung into a parking slot in front of one of the units. Hump drove past. We did a slow tour of Farr Hills. It gave Thompson time to enter his condominium, and it revealed that there was only one way in and out of the development. The way we'd come, through the brick archway.

We waited outside the development, down the road from the archway. We parked on the shoulder next to a construction site where the bunched shells pointed to another apartment complex going up. It was like that all over Atlanta. Boom and bust.

It was twenty after six when the nose of the Continental passed under the archway. It turned and showed its tail to us and sped toward Peachtree Road. I checked the tag numbers. It was the right one.

"Look at that sport."

I did. It was the new Fred Thompson we were staring at in the side parking lot of Sadie Mae's Place. He'd changed from suit and tie to one of those faded denim suits, a black turtleneck, and high-heel boots.

At first, for an instant, I reached for my pad to recheck the tag numbers. The gray hair reassured me. I could follow that head of hair through a snowstorm.

Sadie Mae's is one of the new "in" places on Peachtree Road. A new one opens every three or four months. It booms for a time and then that crowd moves on and another one floats in, getting the scent late. In a year the business falls off and somebody buys the bar. They change the name and some of the decor and a new "in" place is born.

"What drill?"

"Remember the Bill Riley thing?"

"Sure." Hump got out of the Buick. "I'm thirsty. I go first."

I waited a couple of minutes. When I entered the bar, it was wall-to-wall armpits and bodies and elbows. The bar was two-deep, men and women pressed against the stool sitters, and all the tables were taken. A blue smoke haze butted the ceiling.

It was a fight, easing and pushing and snaking my way to the bar for a drink. I got a scotch-rocks and lost some of it on my shoe backing away. I found an empty space along one wall, put my back to it, and looked around.

I found Hump first. He was seated at a table with a black couple. I recognized the black guy as a lawyer with E.O.A. The girl with him looked too young to be his wife. That's Atlanta for you.

Hump's table was near the front end of the bar. His back was to me for a time. Then he looked over his shoulder. His eyes drifted past me like he didn't know me. As planned. But there was something else. I followed the direction of his gaze when he turned away and located Fred Thompson.

Thompson was at a table near the back of the bar. He was to the left of the arch that led to the Men's Room. There were a couple of young chicks with him, the secretary types. He'd have to know them to be sitting with them that soon after entering the bar. I watched the bored, disinterested faces of the girls and decided he was shooting blanks with them.

That hunch got backing. A young stud had been floating near the table. Now he leaned in and said something. The girls laughed and their heads edged together. I flipped from them to Thompson and saw the annoyed look on his face. He put his back to the stud and the girl and tried talking to the girl on his right. But the stud was spreading his light and the girl Thompson spoke to wasn't listening.

Thompson pushed back his chair. I leaned away from the wall. He turned and went through the arch. I'd been to Sadie Mae's one other time and knew the phones were there as well as the john. I clubbed my way through the pack and reached the arch. To the right was the john. To the left a bank of two phones. I dug out a dime.

Thompson was on the left phone. I edged past him and slipped the phone book from the shelf under the phone bank. I stepped back and pretended to flip through the pages. That way I wasn't bothered by the soundboard that separated the two units.

Thompson said: "...like to come by now if I could."

A pause.

"In ten minutes?"

Another pause.

"See you then."

He replaced the receiver and stepped back. He bumped into me and whirled. I said, "Sorry," and stepped around him. I put an elbow on the shelf.

Behind me, Thompson said, "Do I know you?"

I looked at him, "Not that I know."

"You Jim Hardman?"

"Who's that?"

He shook his head and headed for the arch. I dropped in my dime and dialed my number. I let it ring about six times.

I passed his table without looking at him. The young stud was seated at the table. Both girls looked on ready for him. When I passed Hump he was looking up at me. I nodded at him. Even before I got past the table I could hear him begin his "Sorry, but I've got to leave."

I saw a hole at the bar. I drained my glass and pushed my way in. I ordered another scotch-rocks. By the time I paid, Hump had left. The black lawyer from E.O.A. had a hand on the girl's neck.

A minute later Thompson passed me on the way out. I knew he'd stop at the entrance and look back at me. I kept my eyes on the two girls and the stud at the table he'd left. The way the young man had them jollied he was shooting hot loads.

A bit later a girl passed me on the way out. I followed her with my head. Right to the entrance. Thompson was gone. As expected. I returned to the phone and dialed Art's home number. I caught him before he left for his shift at the department. I told him where I'd be. He gave me a maybe. I went back into the bar and wasted ten minutes over my drink.

I left my glass on a table on the way outside. I stood on the curb and flagged down the first cab that passed on my side of Peachtree Road.

The cab dropped me a bit later in front of George's Deli on North Highland. I was having a corned beef and drinking a beer and talking football with the bartender, Sam, when Art sat down next to me. He gave me his now-what-the-hell look.

CHAPTER THIRTEEN

"Next time we do the Bill Riley dance step you'd better remind me where you're going to be," Hump said. "This is the third phone call I've made."

I'd carried my beer bottle to the phone. I had a swallow and braced a hip against the beer box. "Tell me how the P.I. work went."

"You try to spook him?"

"I think he must have seen me around the courthouse some years back. Why?"

"He waited in the parking lot five minutes. Might have been checking to see if you followed him."

"Then?"

"You didn't come out and he drove off. I followed him to a duplex on Ramsay Drive. Had a *For Rent* sign out in the yard. He rang the doorbell. Went in for a few minutes. Came out with another man. The man unlocked the right half of the duplex. They went in, were in there for a time. When they came out the other man was counting some money. Thompson had a key."

"Would that lead you to believe he'd just rented himself another apartment?"

"That would be my trained estimate," Hump said.

"What does he need with another apartment?"

"That's a good question. In fact, this is a bit of a comedown from the place in Farr Hills."

"Could you see him living in a duplex?"

"A sport like him?" Hump laughed.

Art passed the beer box and leaned in. I nodded at him. "Where are you now, Hump?"

"Followed him to his condominium. I think he might be in for the night. I'm at a service station a few blocks from there."

"Hold on a minute." I passed the phone to Art. "Seems Fred Thompson just rented himself half of a duplex on Ramsay Drive. Hump and I can't see him living in that neighborhood."

"I can't either," Art said. Then, into the phone: "Give me that address." Art wrote the numbers down on a margin of the phone book and tore it away. He passed the phone to me. "Want to take a ride, Jim?"

I shook my head. "Hump, I'm going home. Meet me there."

He said he would. I carried my beer down the bar to the end stool and sat down. Art finished his glass and tapped the bar next to me. "What's wrong? You don't want to play detective anymore?"

"Not tonight. I'm tired. You call me."

"All right."

He left. I finished my beer. Then I sipped at another one while Sam made me a roast beef and a corned beef to go. The sandwiches were for Hump. I didn't think he'd found time for a bite yet.

The phone was ringing when I unlocked the door. The living room lights were on. Hump stood in the bedroom doorway and shook his head at me. "I know that call ain't for me."

I dropped the bag of sandwiches in his hands on the way past him. I answered the phone.

"I've been trying to reach you all day," Rosemary said. She sounded stiff-voiced and a little angry.

"It's been busy. I just got home." I switched the phone from hand to hand as I worked my topcoat off. I missed something she said but ran on past it. "We know one new thing. It looks like Billie Joe's gone out of town for a few days."

"Where?"

RALPH DENNIS

I said we didn't know that yet.

"Then how do you know that ...?"

I told her about the arrest of Brian Case. I said that if he knew where Billie Joe was, he wasn't saying.

"I see."

I said I thought he'd talk sooner or later. When he did we'd know.

"You'll let me know, Jim?"

I said that she'd be the first to know.

She waited. There was silence at the other end of the line. I had the sense that she was waiting to see if I'd ask her over or if I'd offer to drive to the Riviera. I didn't do either and finally she said, "Well, let me know."

I said I would and good night.

At the kitchen table Hump was halfway through the roast beef. "You didn't say which sandwich was yours."

I shook my head. "Neither."

"That who I think it was?"

"Yes."

"What did you tell her?"

"I lied some."

"Why, Jim?"

I shrugged. I carried a beer as far as the opener and changed my mind. I put it back in the refrigerator.

"She coming over?"

"I think tomorrow starts early."

"That the reason?"

"No," I said. "I'm afraid the truth might slip out. If we're right about the duplex apartment, why Thompson rented it, then it's going to happen one way or the other. No reason for her to lose a night's sleep over something she can't do anything about."

Hump started on the corned beef. "That's the Hardman I know. Soft and squishy."

I didn't like to think that was true.

He finished eating and left, taking a road beer with him. I watched a bit of TV. I clipped my toe-nails. I was undressed and about ready to give up on Art when he called.

"It looks promising," he said. The owner of the duplex, Arvin Baker, had said that a Mr. Roth had rented the other apartment for his niece and her husband. He'd said that the husband, Bob Johnson, would sign the lease when they moved in the next afternoon.

"You set it up?"

"Baker leaves for work at eight. We'll move in then."

"Give me that address again," I said.

"No way."

"844 Ramsay Drive?"

"Shit," Art said.

"See you at eight." I broke the connection.

The lights were off and I was in bed before I remembered that I hadn't changed the sheets. Rosemary's smell was in the sheets and the pillow. I was too tired to care. I slept well and if I dreamed at all, I didn't remember any of it.

I'd set my mental clock. I awoke exactly at 6:30.

I arrived at the duplex on Ramsay Drive exactly at eight. Art's car was in the drive. He answered the door and waved me in. Ellison was seated in an easy chair that had been positioned near the window. He was drinking coffee from a large paper cup and eating an egg sandwich.

"What happened to what's-his-name?"

"Baker? He left for work." Art dug into a paper bag and passed me a cup of coffee. "We were afraid you'd show up."

I took the cup and pried the top away. "What's the drill?"

"This." Art passed me a piece of paper. I read enough of it to see that it was one of the standard-lease agreements you could buy at most of the business-supply stores. "I'm Arvin Baker for the day."

"Who am I?"

"Nobody," Ellison said. "You're a bystander."

"Goody." I let the swallow of coffee I took serve as a beat. "Like yesterday?"

Ellison said, "Jesus Christ." He shoved the rest of his egg sandwich into his mouth and stared out the window at the street.

Ellison didn't stay mad long. It wasn't in his nature. As the day went on, I learned a good bit about him. His first name was Bill and he was married and he had two little girls. He'd been hoping for a boy each time and now he wasn't sure he could afford another baby. "All I got was splittails," he said about his little girls, but he talked with affection and pride about how bright they were.

I got to learn all that because they couldn't decide exactly what to do with me. The drill they'd set was for two positions. Art in the duplex. Ellison outside in a car across the street. In the end they decided I could do less damage if I waited in the car with Ellison.

It was a long afternoon. After they checked out the walkie-talkies there wasn't much to do. I remembered there was a transistor radio in the glove compartment of my Ford. We listened to shit-kicker music until the batteries died around five. A time later, a 1973 blue Mustang with a dented right-rear fender pulled into the driveway behind Art's car.

"That's Baker," Ellison said.

Art met Baker on the walk. After they talked a bit, Baker got back into the Mustang and drove away. Art returned to the duplex. Over the walkie-talkie he explained that he'd sent Baker to supper and a movie.

It was that way, dull and slow, until almost seven. It was going toward full dark when the 1957 Mercury eased down the street toward us. Slowing, stopping. Starting up again. Even before it stopped in front of the duplex I tapped Ellison on the shoulder. "That's it."

Ellison spoke into the walkie-talkie. "Incoming, Art."

Art said he'd seen it.

Billie Joe opened the door on the driver's side and stepped out. The inside overhead light flashed on her blond hair when she leaned into the backseat. The light also revealed that the passenger seat was empty.

I grabbed the walkie-talkie. "It looks like she's alone, Art."

"I'll play it the best I can," Art said. "I'll call back."

Across the street, Billie Joe dragged out one suitcase and then a second one. Balancing them, struggling with them, she went up the walk. About the time she placed them on the single porch that served both halves of the duplex, the porch light flared on.

I could see the girl better in the strong light. It was the girl I'd seen in the 7–11 a few nights before. The light didn't bother her. She fumbled in her shoulder bag and brought out a key with a tag on it.

Art joined her on the porch. They gestured and talked and then Art took the key from her and went to the other apartment. He opened the door and carried her bags in for her. The door closed behind them, Art came out two or three minutes later. He didn't look toward us. He entered the Baker apartment. Within seconds he was on the walkie-talkie.

"Bill? Jim?"

Ellison took the walkie-talkie from me. "Here."

"That's only one fish. I want the other one too."

"How?"

"She says her husband will sign the lease when he gets here. She says she's leaving to pick him up in a minute."

"Where's he supposed to be?"

"She didn't say."

The door to the other apartment opened. Billie Joe stepped out and pulled the door closed behind her. "She's outside now," Ellison said.

"You follow," Art said. "I'll be half a block behind."

"Dammit," Ellison hissed at me. "I was supposed to call a backup and now I don't know what to do."

"Best laid plans," I said.

Billie Joe pulled the Mercury into the driveway behind Art's car. When she backed out again, turning, both Ellison and I ducked our heads. As soon as the headlights passed, Ellison started the engine. We gave her half a block and eased in behind her. Two blocks away from the duplex the car behind us hit his brights. It told us that Art was in position.

We played leapfrog across town. It was drill in case she was watching her rearview mirror. We'd give way to Art and he'd play lead car for a few blocks and then give it back to us.

"Where the hell is she going?" Ellison asked me.

I shrugged.

We were lead car, Art a distance behind us, when I saw her pump her brakes and slow. I didn't know exactly where we were. It wasn't a neighborhood I knew.

The Mercury turned left off the street. "Slow," I told Ellison. We passed a large building that housed an antique shop and then I saw the Mercury. It was parked in front of a Stop and Shop store. The headlights of the Mercury lit up a heavy-set man who stepped out of a pay-phone booth and walked toward the passenger side of the car. It was, I thought, the other young man we'd been looking for. Bob Buchner. The window on the passenger side had been rolled down. Buchner reached in. When he backed away, he held something wrapped in a dark piece of cloth.

Just past the Stop and Shop store, a street forked to the left. Ellison made it without squealing the tires. "What's going on?" He braked the car as soon as the building masked us.

"You know how broke you are when you come back from a vacation?"

He understood it.

I hit the walkie-talkie button. "Art, these assholes are pulling a job."

"I'll come from the antique shop side."

"Right." I dropped the walkie-talkie on the seat and got out. Ellison met me at the rear of the car and caught my arm.

"Where you going?"

"I think I can take the girl out. Count to twenty slow." I jerked my arm free. I moved away before he could argue.

When I looked back, he was checking his piece for loads.

CHAPTER FOURTEEN

I passed the front of the store without looking in. I had my head down, like the wind and the sand blowing in it was bothering me. When I was level with the Mercury, I lifted the hem of my topcoat and fumbled with a handful of change. I separated a couple of quarters and left the rest in my pocket. I reached the phone booth, started in, and then turned and stared down at the quarters in my hand.

The Mercury engine was running. It ran rough, as if there might be one cylinder missing. I listened to the engine and did my best parody of the poor cluck who didn't have a dime. I was counting to myself. The count reached fifteen. I stepped to the window on the driver's side and tapped the window with one of the quarters.

She rolled the window down a couple of inches. I said, "Lady, you got change for a quarter?"

"No."

"You sure?" I reached twenty. I looked to see if the lock button was down. It wasn't. My right hand dropped and gripped the door handle.

"Yes, I'm sure. How about leaving me ...?"

I looked over my shoulder. Art was coming up behind me. Then I saw Ellison. He'd been slower with his count. He rounded the far end of the store building and stopped to light a smoke.

It was set. I backed away. The door came open. I stepped around the door and rammed myself into the car. The light was on and I could see her wide, surprised eyes before I fell on top of her. The wheel caught me on the shoulder. I twisted past that. She squirmed and raised a knee. There went one ball and the pain sliced up my side. But the turning she'd done had stretched her out beneath me, front to front. I almost laughed. It was like some grotesque teenage drive-in movie coupling.

I felt her trying to slip from under me. She freed her right hand and seemed to be reaching for something. I realized she was groping for the horn. I caught that arm and pressed it down. But her left hand was free, digging past my shoulder. The hand became a claw. It missed my eye but raked my face.

Behind me, at the door, Art said, "Move your feet." I did. He closed the door and the overhead light went out.

Beneath me, I could feel her filling her lungs. "Go ahead and scream. He'll walk right into it."

The breath hissed away.

"Keep her still," Art said.

"Damn you, damn you." She gave it up. She relaxed and turned into jelly.

"Here's our boy," Art whispered. Then he shouted: "Police, Buchner. Hands over your head and don't move."

The silence. I thought it was over. Ellison, from a distance straight ahead, yelled, "Drop the piece, Buchner."

I lifted my head. I got my eyes to a level with the bottom of the passenger window. I saw Bob Buchner on the curb just outside the door to the store. The squarish, blocky piece in his right hand looked like a .45 automatic. There was a wad of bills in the other hand. I saw him look toward the Mercury. Then he whirled and lunged for the door. He was going back inside.

Art and Ellison fired within split seconds of each other. The slugs hit Buchner in the back and the side and drove him against the door. Glass shattered. Beneath me, Billie Joe screamed. It was a breathless scream, almost a whisper.

Bob Buchner, dead or dying, became a doorstop.

Art cuffed Billie Joe's hands behind her. He looked past her shoulder. "I think she got you, Jim."

I ran a hand over the right side of my face. The fingers came away bloody.

"It's like that," I said. "Some days you can't make a penny."

Billie Joe braced her butt against the front fender of the Mercury. She hadn't taken her eyes off me since I yanked her out of the car. "You fat turd," she said.

She tried to spit on me but the wind blew it back at her.

I made the call from the payphone. I reached Hump at his apartment. He'd been waiting all day.

"The girl's not hurt. Buchner's dead. They'll be taking Billie Joe to the station and booking her. You deal with Rosemary. Call her and tell her. See if she knows a lawyer in Atlanta. If she doesn't, call Rod Carswell at home. Tell him he owes us a favor and that the Atkinsons can pay his fee. It might be the Atkinsons will want their own lawyer later, but she ought to be represented by somebody now."

"You'll be there?"

"I'm out of it as of now." I looked at the crowd of gawkers that were collecting at the storefront. "This goes to trial, I'll be the number-one witness against the girl. It might be better if we do it this way. With everybody involved."

"Rosemary too?"

"Especially her." I opened the door to the phone booth. The cold wind sucked at me. "Hell, it's your case anyway. You took it on, you get to tie up the loose ends."

"Where'll you be?"

"Around," I said. "Christmas shopping."

The paddy wagon was on the way. It was due. I stopped near Art. He'd been talking to Billie Joe while I'd been on the phone. "She wants her lawyer," Art said.

"Your mother will be at the station by the time you get there. She'll arrange for a lawyer."

"You know my mother?"

"The Dragonlady?" I watched her face change. "I know her."

"I want my own lawyer," Billie Joe said.

"Fred Thompson? He won't be available."

"He needs a lawyer himself," Art said.

I stepped closer to Billie Joe. "Answer me a question."

"You can ask it."

"How did Fred Thompson fit into this?"

"He's been helping me."

"Why?"

"The usual reasons." The tone was dry, bitter.

"Which are?"

"What reasons do repulsive old men have?"

"Those?" I said.

"Those. He was a nasty old man. A sickening old man." Her head turned. She looked at Bill Ellison and at the uniformed cops who'd arrived minutes after the shooting and then at Art and me. "Just like you, all of you are pigs."

"No," I said. "I'm an ex-pig."

I did my Christmas shopping in some out of the way, rat-suck bars. I didn't see anything I wanted to buy for Marcy. Hump was easier to shop for. I saw a blonde that I wanted to gift wrap for him.

Somewhere around two a.m. I was in a bar on West Peachtree, close in toward downtown. A slim girl with black hair and a northern accent was telling me all the wonderful, exotic things she'd do for me for "five-oh" dollars, all the time playing with my skinned knees. I said that I didn't think that was very remarkable. If you put two snakes in a burlap bag…or two goats…or two monkeys…

"Fat man?"

I looked up and saw Hump. He looked cold sober. That told me that he hadn't been checking all the bars searching for me. My guess was that he'd driven through a lot of parking lots near bars, until he found my Ford.

"Ready to pack it in?"

"Hey," the girl with dark hair protested, "we're having fun."

A slick hard-ass at the bar who'd been watching the girl and me for the last hour eased off the bar stool and said, "He's old enough to vote, he's old enough to decide if he wants to drink."

Hump put his left hand under my armpit and pulled me out of the chair. His eyes remained on the hard-ass. "No jackrolling tonight," he said. "Maybe some other night."

I was walking better than I thought I could. Hump gave me a soft push that started me for the front door.

The slick hard-ass said, "I don't think I like that remark."

"Fuck what you like or don't like," Hump said.

I looked over my shoulder and turned. Hump short-punched the guy. He went down with his head against the base of one of the bar stools. His heels jerked and squeaked on the tile floor.

On the street the cold air revived me. I said, "That's fun, Hump. Let's do one more jackroller."

"Tomorrow." Hump caught my arm and turned me toward the parking lot. "Tomorrow's a better day for it."

We reached the car. He put me into the passenger side of his Buick and got behind the wheel. "I guess you're wondering why I came looking for you?"

"Yeah."

He started the engine and backed out of the lot. "I wanted to remind you there is one more shopping day until Christmas."

"One day?"

"That's right."

"One day." I closed my eyes. He drove me home.

THE END

AFTERWORD

Jim Hardman, The First Truly Hardboiled Private Eye
By Mel Odom

I found my first Hardman novel, *The Charleston Knife's Back In Town*, in a 7–11 spinner rack in the summer of 1974. It was the second in the series and I couldn't find the first, so that bothered me some because I'm a completest with OCD tendencies.

The cover was interesting enough that I picked the book up anyway. I wasn't ready for it, and after I finished it and was suitably jarred by the jagged edges and violence, I didn't get back to the series for a few years.

I worked at the service station across the street with my dad. I was sixteen and impressionable, still trying to find out who I was as a person and struggling with how I was going to be a writer. I figured I had a lot of strikes against me: born in Oklahoma, worked at a service station to help the family, and wrangled pigs because my dad insisted on raising them. Probably because his father did when he was a kid. I didn't have any of the interesting jobs writers seemed to have. I didn't know it at the time, but I was collecting lots of interesting story material and getting to know folks who would come to people them.

I was getting fifty cents an hour at the time. Since books were about a buck and comics had climbed to the ungodly price of *twenty cents an issue!,* I could work my shift and pick up a book or two or a fistful of comics. Summers were great because I worked six days a week from eight to five. That was four dollars a day I could spend on books and comics. It was a benchmark for me back in those days. My peers weren't interested in those things.

By that time I was reading nearly everything Pinnacle was doing. I picked up novels about the Executioner, the Destroyer, and every other *-er* that came out. The only things I knew at that age was that I wanted to be a writer and I wanted true love. I blame Edgar Rice Burroughs's John Carter of Mars books for the latter.

I loved private eye fiction. At least, I thought I did. I'd read the Continental Op stories, *The Maltese Falcon,* and Raymond Chandler's Philip Marlowe novels. I also perused old copies of *Ellery Queen's Mystery Magazine, Alfred Hitchcock's Mystery Magazine,* and *Mike Shayne's Mystery Magazine* I bought for fifteen cents a copy from the mom-and-pop grocery store on the corner diagonal from the 7–11.

I wanted to grow up and write private eye fiction. Now, with over two hundred novels written under my name and various pseudonyms, I still haven't written a private eye novel. I still want to.

At the time I picked up that Hardman book, I thought I knew private eye and mystery stories.

I didn't.

I thought the books were going to be another of those *-er* series where the violence was so over the top it all seemed like fantasy.

They weren't.

Hardman lived in a meaner, more real, and more violent world than anything I'd ever known or imagined. I'd grown up on movies where bad guys got shot and fell down. Their heads didn't explode. And good guys were good guys, men you could place money on to do the right thing no matter what. I hadn't yet seen Clint Eastwood in action as Dirty Harry even though the first and second movies were out. The only Sam Peckinpah movies I'd seen had been cleaned up for television.

Hardman was billed as "a great new private eye for the shockproof '70s" on the back covers of several of the books and in interior advertisements.

I wasn't shockproof. I drowned in the coarse language, the graphic violence, and some of the decidedly unheroic qualities of the character.

I finished the book, because I always did back in those days, and put it on the shelf. I didn't return to the series until I was married and nineteen years old. Yep, older and wiser—and way less innocent. Those things made a difference.

Working at a service station and raising pigs while maintaining an otherwise isolated existence left me feeling that Hardman and Hump Evans lived in a world I couldn't hope to understand. I didn't even want to be part of it as a reader.

Getting married, going to college, and being forced into a larger worldview changed my understanding of how the world truly worked. By that year, 1977, we'd gone through the New York City Blackout, David Berkowitz—the Son of Sam—had been arrested as a serial killer, Rocky had said, "Cut me, Mick," when his eyes were swollen shut and we saw the blood spurt on the big screen, and Elvis died.

That year the Hardman series were up to nearly all of the books that would be published. It was also all over the racks of the bookstores.

I hunted down the first book and read it. I'd changed and was more accepting of the violence in Hardman's world.

I burned through the novels at that point. Couldn't get enough of them. Thankfully they were easy to find and I was working at a job where I had more money (big upgrade from fifty cents an hours to $2.32—minimum wage was only $2.10 at the time).

Although I wasn't ready for my first read of *The Charleston Knife's Back In Town*, I re-read it when I plunged into the series and loved it. I loved it so much that I glued that book's cover back on *twice*. Those old Pyramid Books paperbacks were pretty shoddily produced at times. In fact, it wasn't until the eighth book, *The Deadly Cotton Heart*, that I stopped worrying about cracking the glue along the spine when I opened the book—and that was when I bought it new!

Ada, Oklahoma, was the big town near where I grew up in Francis, Oklahoma, population 332. At twelve thousand strong and a university town, Ada was a lot bigger than anywhere I'd thought I would live.

Ada was also extremely segregated, not too surprising in the 1970s. Civil Rights movements were still taking place. When you grow up in that environment you're of two minds. If you want to stay small town and segregated, you think you know everything you need to. I didn't. One of the high school janitors, Mr. Hightower, was African-American and talked to me. I was pure white trash and helped raise hogs. He told me he took that job at the high school so he could be close to his two sons. And from everything I saw, he was. He impressed me and that feeling stuck.

I played basketball at school and joined pickup games at the local gyms, so I knew a lot of the African-American guys who did the same. Growing up in that environment made it hard to get to know each other, though, because everybody kept walls up.

I think that's one of the reasons I enjoyed Hump Evans in the Hardman series. I knew guys like him. Guys who were college stars but couldn't make it to the Bigs for one reason or another and sometimes played South American Pan-Am leagues, and were still trying to figure out where they were going to go from there. We were all incredibly young then. I know some of them didn't do well after that, and there were a lot of sad stories and some not so sad along the way. Those stories are in every color and every culture, but they spoke to me then.

As I recall, Hump is in every Hardman novel, but we never knew much about him outside of him being ex-NFL with a knee that took him a step off his best game, six feet six inches tall, and two hundred seventy pounds. So when *Hump's First Case* came out, I was excited by the promise of learning more about the character.

Hump's First Case delivers some of that, but not as much as I'd wanted. It presents more of the dynamic that made Hardman and Hump work as a team, and why they were together. Atlanta was, and is, a black and white city with a Southern bent. Except for technological advancements, some pop culture additions, and some re-zoning, I think Atlanta remains what it was: a city in constant motion trying to figure out where the balance is.

The author's efforts to pen authentic dialogue to represent the times he was writing in, as well as the underbelly of Atlanta, is pretty dead on from what I recall of the times. Of course, times have changed and some readers might be offended at the way Dennis handles black and white relationships and women. But I'd caution everyone to remember that these books are just representative of those days, much as Edgar Rice Burroughs's depiction of black nations in the Tarzan novels.

At the heart of the Hardman series are two guys, one white, one black, who strive to make their way in a harsh and unforgiving world. Dennis's stripped-down prose, his unflinching look at the way things were and the way people comported themselves, his bare knuckles approach to crime and criminals, all of those things prepared me as a writer to write cleanly and honestly.

I've still got the original paperbacks in a storage unit where I've got a treasure trove of books I'll probably never live long enough to see again. I think about them every now and again, and I promise myself I'll dig them out. Thankfully Brash Books is bringing out these new digital editions and trade paperbacks so I can simply add them to my Kindle and re-read them, which I plan to do.

Often, you can't go back and read a novel you read forty years ago and enjoy it. Most of you who discover these books now are simply too young to have known them when they first came out. And many times so much has changed about the world or changed about you that the read just doesn't even come close to that first experience. *Hump's First Case* does. And I'm betting all the other books do too.

I just wish Brash Books had more of the series to reprint. They were gone far too soon.

Mel Odom is the Alex Award-winning author of *The Rover* and has written over two hundred novels in the fantasy, science fiction, and adventure genres. His tie-in novels include books in the *Buffy the Vampire Slayer, Sabrina the Teenage Witch*, and Wizards of the Coast's Forgotten Realms. You can learn more about him at www.melodombooks.com

ABOUT THE AUTHOR

Ralph Dennis isn't a household name...but he should be. He is widely considered among crime writers as a master of the genre, denied the recognition he deserved because his twelve *Hardman* books, which are beloved and highly sought-after collectables now, were poorly packaged in the 1970s by Popular Library as a cheap men's action-adventure paperbacks with numbered titles.

Even so, some top critics saw past the cheesy covers and noticed that he was producing work as good as John D. MacDonald, Raymond Chandler, Chester Himes, Dashiell Hammett, and Ross MacDonald.

The *New York Times* praised the *Hardman* novels for "expert writing, plotting, and an unusual degree of sensitivity. Dennis has mastered the genre and supplied top entertainment." The *Philadelphia Daily News* proclaimed *Hardman* "the best series around, but they've got such terrible covers..."

Unfortunately, Popular Library didn't take the hint and continued to present the series like hack work, dooming the novels to a short shelf-life and obscurity...except among generations of crime writers, like novelist Joe R. Lansdale (the *Hap & Leonard* series) and screenwriter Shane Black (the *Lethal Weapon* movies), who've kept Dennis' legacy alive through word-of-mouth and by acknowledging his influence on their stellar work.

Ralph Dennis wrote three other novels that were published outside of the *Hardman* series but he wasn't able to reach the wide audience, or gain the critical acclaim, that he deserved during his lifetime.

He was born in 1931 in Sumter, South Carolina, and received a masters degree from University of North Carolina, where he later taught film and television writing after serving a stint in the Navy. At the time of his death in 1988, he was working at a bookstore in Atlanta and had a file cabinet full of unpublished novels.

Brash Books will be releasing the entire *Hardman* series, his three other published novels, and his long-lost manuscripts.

www.ingramcontent.com/pod-product-compliance
Lightning Source LLC
Chambersburg PA
CBHW021233020726
47498CB00008B/2823